Puffin Books

Editor: Kaye Webb

Leon

The puppy howled and felt the hot gushing of his
own blood and began to whimper again, no longer
even trying to escape. With one more blow the
crow would destroy him. . . . But that blow never
comes. Instead he feels the gentle hands of Hilario,
the farm boy with a dream of being a doctor.

But as Leon grows into a magnificent creature of
strength and courage, his life and fortunes change.
His young master is forced to sell him to Don
Agustín, the local landowner, but the rich man
cannot buy his loyalty or love and the pair are briefly
reunited.

Then comes the horror of the Spanish Civil War and
Leon is left starving and bewildered. His new master
savagely ill-treats him and he becomes an outlaw,
killing the sheep it was once his pride to protect.

A vivid and moving story for readers of ten to
thirteen.

Cover design by Victor Ambrus

D0785578

Helen Griffiths

Leon

Illustrated by Victor G. Ambrus

Penguin Books
in association with Hutchinson of London

Penguin Books Ltd, Harmondsworth,
Middlesex, England
Penguin Books Australia Ltd, Ringwood,
Victoria, Australia

First published by Hutchinson Junior Books 1967
Published in Puffin Books 1972

Copyright © Helen Griffiths 1967
Illustrations copyright © Hutchinson & Co. (Publishers) Ltd, 1967

Made and printed in Great Britain by
Richard Clay (The Chaucer Press) Ltd,
Bungay, Suffolk
Set in Monotype Bembo

Contents

1: Birth and death

The summer of 1933 was as hot as any on the bare Castilian
plain. In the distance the heat shimmered, seeming as much to
rise from the achingly hot earth as to beat down from the
almost cloudless sky. There were no trees on the plain, only
stunted bushes and patches of wiry grass. There were also
long, long stretches of ripening wheat, the heavy ears drooping
on the stiff dry stalks, and there was hardly a breeze to scratch
among the corn. Between the unfenced yellow rectangles
which patterned the red and white and grey countryside were
the scarred traces of an arid watercourse with a few tough
wild flowers withering reluctantly on the hardly distinguish-
able banks; the narrow tracks made by man and beast; a few
giant boulders, grey and shapeless, which by rights belonged
to wilder ground than this and seemed to come by accident
upon this diligently cultivated area which stretched to hilly
horizons.

It was only the burnishing wheat and the cart-tracks that

told of the existence of man somewhere beyond this emptiness. The wheat could not grow alone and the tracks had to
lead to somewhere. They went to a village, small and as
unexpected as the boulders, hardly visible in the sunlight, as
drab and as dusty as the colourless earth, crushed into nothing
by the immensity of the gently undulating plains and the
fierce blueness of the sky.

The village had come into being centuries earlier because
of the stream that trickled endlessly over a flat bed of rocks
only a short distance away. Grass never had much opportunity
to grow on its banks, for every day women came to wash
clothes, men came with thirsty animals, children came to
play. The ground had grown hard and barren. The thirsty
earth and sun sucked up whatever drops of water fell upon it.
Within two minutes of its falling, the ground was once again
dry.

It was a poor village. There were some thirty houses,
granite built, some taller than others but never more than two
storeys topped by faded red tiles. There was a church, larger
than the houses but only just, its bell tower claiming the
existence of a village from a distance. The men of the village
worked in the fields, which they owned or rented; the women
worked in the houses except for when they were on the river
bank washing the clothes and hanging them out to dry.

Each house had a small yard which would shelter a pig, a
few chickens, perhaps a mule or a pair of oxen. The yards
were thick with straw which would later be spread on the
exhausted earth to fertilize it. In many of the yards a dog was
tied, usually a large animal of uncertain breed and most
certain ferociousness. They were nameless dogs and half forgotten. They spent their lives in sleeping, scratching and bored
wakefulness, only roused by the approach of a stranger, a
stranger being anyone who was not their master.

Not all the dogs of the village were tied. There was always
a number of them, both ownerless and owned, that wandered

freely about, scrounging the smallest edible matter be it bone or beetle. The weak ones tried to attach themselves to a friendly lad; the clever ones were independent. The weak ones fed more often but were subject to various indignities and could never be certain of their masters' will; the independent ones were noble or cunning, according to their individual natures.

The large, tawny bitch that looked something like a collie, with her long slender muzzle, soft, semi-pricked ears and heavy ruff, was noble by nature. Her size commanded respect from the smaller mongrels, for, though she rarely demeaned herself to battle over a stone-hard crust of bread, bold was the dog that would dispute it with her. Were she not so tatteringly thin beneath the matted rug of hair that covered her, she would have been a handsome animal, with dark eyes that were never craven even when she sat for two hours just beyond the boot reach of a man eating a hunk of bread and blood sausage.

She did not beg with her eyes nor with her starving frame. She just sat and hardly looked at him, knowing that patience would surely triumph if she were not driven away at the beginning. Often the last crust would be tossed to her, sometimes two or three, according to the mood or the heart of the man. When the crust landed fairly between herself and the man, near to his reach, she would not go for it. She had learned not to do that from painful experience. The bread would stay on the ground, sweet-smelling and appetizing until the man went away or until, admiring her good sense, it might be ruefully retrieved by its owner and tossed under her nose.

Most of her sustenance came from the rubbish dump to the south of the village. She had learned to avoid broken glass and sardine tins and nuzzled gingerly through ashes, dust, discarded sandals, swallowing all that was slightly edible before trotting down to a place by the stream where she could drink undisturbed. She would then look for a shadow. Her favourite spot was beneath an abandoned farm-cart where she could snuffle for insects while escaping the sun, her tongue dripping sweat from her open jaws, her skeleton frame panting in the heat. Eventually she would sleep. Hunger would make her growl; fleas caused her to twitch and a back leg would saw the air involuntarily. Only while sleeping did her dignity desert her and she became as any other dog, a lowly masterless mongrel.

Twice a year the collie-like mongrel produced puppies. There were two or three in each litter, varying in size and colouring, but not in feebleness nor the instinct to live. Of each litter at least one would die within a day or two of its birth. She always knew instinctively which it would be and ignored it after the first licking. Its brothers or sisters would push it aside in their own struggles to gain the life that came from the mother flank; it would be thrust farther and farther away by their determined wrigglings and soon the cold little body would become icy, frozen to eternal immobility.

Few of the bitch's offspring survived the first months of life. So many pitfalls awaited them, the greatest of which was hunger. Then there was man who had to be avoided at all costs, for at times there were puppies all over the village and it could not support them. A shadow falling over them while they slept or half-heartedly played, a relentless hand gripping them by the scruff; the cold shock of water from which they could not escape, filling their nostrils, mouths, ears and lungs. The mother dog was never surprised when her offspring were snatched from her. It had happened so many times and she knew better than to question the will of man.

It was her knowledge of man and his ways which had kept her alive for eight years already, so close to his sudden cruelty or occasional kindness. She had learned to expect both and to divine as accurately as possible with her intelligent but limited animal brain how to avoid one and take advantage of the other. She was not an unhappy dog. Her miserable state was the only one that she had ever known and it was as natural to her as the moon that puzzled her and the sun she avoided.

There were occasions of unexpected pleasure, usually on the discovery of a bone she could gnaw at for hours and deceive the hunger that always niggled. There were moments of utter misery, caused by pain, hunger or cold, or all three together. But mostly she went about her business of survival with plumy tail held high and sometimes wagging, just being alive a good reason for joy.

2

On a day in July of 1933, some time in the afternoon when the sun was at its most insistent, the tawny bitch was unhappy. She had sought the shelter of the broken-down cart, rotting slowly at the edge of a field not far from the village, panting and anxious, knowing from the experience of many years that soon, very soon, there would be a new litter of younglings, squirming blindly to her for protection. She had had no energy all the day to search for food. As she grew older and bonier each whelping took a greater toll, and greater than pain was weakness. Weakness she instinctively feared. She knew it was the beginning of the end. Only strength could keep a starving dog alive.

Her strength seemed to wane as the heat increased. The farm-cart was her only refuge, the place she had known as home for many a year, and she had come to it instinctively. But the heat was in the ground as well as in the sky and the sun's rays pierced through cracks in the rotted woodwork. The big mongrel's thirst grew and she panted and perspired, flaying her withers and thin back with the sweat from her jaws, but she was too far from the river to drag her aching body to its edge.

She closed her dark eyes and stretched her jaws across her hindlegs, shutting her mouth occasionally as she dozed but quickly opening it again to pant some more. Eventually the sun passed over, swathing shadows in its wake, square, uneven patches in the village, long cloud shadows over the cornfields. In the first coolness of the late afternoon the mongrel's last puppies were born, two tawny-coloured creatures like herself, appearing almost black-coated in the dampness of the hair. They had blunt clumsy noses, floppy ears, and the small heads were thick with big wrinkles which almost hid the sealed eye slits completely.

There were two of them only and the mother's smooth tongue licked and pummelled until they were almost dry, the hair fluffed softly over the round frames. With weak limbs they levered themselves close to the warmth that would shelter them, nuzzling eagerly under the hot flank until they found the milk they sought. While they sucked and spluttered industriously, the mother continued to lick and sniff. One was slightly bigger than the other, slightly stronger, slightly more dominant. It was the dog puppy and the mother gave him an extra caress as if to let him know that he was the one she favoured.

Suddenly the hungry mouths were hungry no more and the hot tongues slipped tiredly away. The two blind heads pushed close to the mother and she wound herself around them and slept with them, feeling no hunger now, no weakness, feeling only maternal pride and contentment.

She slept all through the night with them, hardly stirring except for once when they awoke again in search of more milk which she eagerly gave. The night was warm but there was a breeze that crept through the corn stalks and tumbled over the barren places. It tugged at the tawny mongrel's matted coat, slightly chilling her back, but it could not reach the puppies almost suffocated beneath her.

By morning the breeze had gone, absorbed by the sun. There was only heat, new hunger for the puppies, great hunger for the mother dog. She was suddenly exhausted again, with hardly the energy to drag herself from under the cart. She was loath to leave the puppies and when she got up from them and moved away they whimpered and wriggled and searched for her blindly, legs scrabbling helplessly. Then they found each other and sought mutual comfort in each other's warmth. They were still and silent again and the mother dog no longer watched them.

She stood with legs spread wide apart, her back sunken. In a day and a night she had lost all her energy; the pups and the heat had sucked it away. She wanted only a drink of water, but the stream was far away. A fly settled on her muzzle. She let it stay there and it moved up to her head. She caught sight of two boys gambolling about not far away. They shouted and waved sticks at each other and this was enough to make her forgo the badly needed water and return to the pups, afraid for them.

She did not venture again from under the cart until night-fall and she felt the weakness creeping within her. It grew each time the puppies sucked at her, leaving her body exhausted and dry, but until the coolness of the night had come she was too much afraid for the puppies to desert them. It was late. The moon was high in the sky, almost a full moon, which fell brilliantly over the countryside and silhouetted every stalk and post and donkey in the yard. The humans were all asleep, or at least in their houses, when the mongrel went down to the stream to drink.

It took her a long time and only thirst drove her. Her weary body fought against the thirst and she tarded long in reaching the bank. When she got there she swayed and almost fell, and waited to regain her balance before approaching the water closely.

The stream ran swiftly at that part and fairly deep. The mongrel's head was reflected in the water, broken and deformed by the ripples she caused as she lapped noisily, desperately, as if her thirst could never be satisfied. But at last the

burning throat was cool and the aching stomach partially satisfied. She had no wish to seek for food and hunger was gradually leaving her. Now that she had reached the water she was
loath to leave it and might not have done so had not the
memory of her lonely puppies compelled her.

There was a breeze again and on the breeze was the faint
hint of a hare not far away, perhaps hidden in the corn that
encroached the cart-track she followed. Days ago it would
have made her ears prick and her body quiver; she would
have been in the corn in search of it, despite the whiskers that
would cling to her ears and stick in her eyes. She would not
have caught it but its tempting nearness and the thought
of it would have been enough to set the plumy tail to wave.

Within a few days all her strength had gone. It seemed that
in giving life to two new beings she had deprived herself of
her own. Even an upturned beetle, wearily gesticulating its
helplessness with six legs right under her nose, did not interest
her. Days ago she would have swallowed it still kicking.
Now she did not even sniff at it, but turned her gaze away
as if the sight of it molested her.

She quickened her pace as she neared the pups. They were
her only interest now; her only reason for existence. Blind,
they were unaware of her presence until they felt her closeness
and then they grew whimperingly excited, their distended
stomachs and fat haunches wriggling their delight, and they
grabbed at her with eager mouths hardly before she could
stretch herself comfortably beside them. The bitch puppy
yelped as she trod on its tail.

Suddenly the mother dog no longer knew what she was
doing. She sprang jerkily to all fours again, snapping at the
puppies that pulled on her, the dark eyes glazing as uncontrollable movements convulsed her. She fell to the ground,
uttering choking noises, her open jaws flecked with foam. A
moment later she was up again to begin a series of short dashes
in different directions. Her movements were blind and blun-

dering. Once she crashed her head against the cart but was unaware of it. The puppies listened to the frantic movements of the mother dog, cringing together, instinctively afraid.

The movements stopped and they heard the exhausted bitch pant, growling and whimpering, terrified by the thing that possessed her. Her legs gave way at last and she squirmed for a while before stretching out her head and neck in one long, last spasm as life suddenly deserted her.

When she was silent and still the two bereft puppies under the cart began to whimper.

2: Orphan

By the time the sun had crushed the early-morning freshness
from the sky the next day the flies were droning busily near
the farm-cart. The noise of them woke the two puppies,
huddled with their muzzles in each other's haunches. They
woke with ravenous hunger and whimpered persistently for
the mother dog, then they began to search each other's hot,
tight bodies, but sucking a mouthful of hair or a jutting
elbow only made them hungrier. They began to grow angry
with each other, pummelling with cross muzzles and clumsy
paws, when suddenly they were flattened to the ground by
a terrible cry which seemed to tear apart the small bit of world
they knew. The cry came again, wild, shrieking, triumphant,

and they cowered in abject fear, crushing themselves to the earth, forgetting hunger, forgetting each other, silent and unmoving.

A big black crow, as shiny as the buzzing flies, had perched on one of the cart shafts, eyeing the carcass of the mother dog. It sidled up and down the shaft, head on one side, and occasionally it opened its large beak to shrill to its not-far-distant companions. Then, assured of the dog's immobility, it flapped to the ground and stalked up to join the flies.

There were soon five or six crows within the vicinity of the abandoned farm-cart, noisy, quarrelsome, flapping their huge wings, tearing at each other, screeching and cawing. They were too occupied with the prey they had already discovered to think of searching for more and the two puppies remained unnoticed, crushed against the back end of the cart which was almost a part of the ground on which it rested, so long had it been there. It was a dark spot, as comforting to them as any place could be that morning, with the noise of the carrion birds so close. Their shivering backs were pressed against hard wood; their hollow stomachs touched the soft ground. They were too afraid to move or to whimper and their hiding-place stayed secret.

The crows did not go away. Their craws full, they perched on the cart and dozed in the hot sunshine. There was no sign of life anywhere to disturb them. The cart was well away from the village and only rarely did someone walk that way. For this reason the mother dog had chosen the spot for her puppies. The puppies knew that the crows were still there although no more screeches were sounded to convulse them with fear. The farm-cart creaked under the weight and the slight movement of them; there was a rustle of wing feathers and claw scratching against beak.

The long afternoon slowly passed. The silence was as heavy as the heat. The puppies were still too frightened to feel hunger. They ached for the presence of the mother dog and could not understand why she did not come, although they were too afraid to whimper for her or to make the slightest movement in search of her. With the tardy arrival of the evening, the crows flapped away, noisy again. Coolness came; the long, slow relief of cool silence. The two puppies uncrushed themselves from their now exceedingly uncomfortable position and, lacking the mother dog, began to suck at each other again, making loud noises in their frustration.

They slept very little that night and no longer found comfort in each other. The bitch puppy was already growing cold and was static, making no complaint when her brother pulled roughly at her nor caring when he left her completely alone. The dog puppy had lost some of his fear and wriggled about questingly for a long time, sniffing, listening, but understanding nothing. Hunger kept him from being still like his sister. It was beginning to dominate everything, even his fear. He wriggled right away from the nesting place with his sister and eventually gave up the struggle in exhaustion, falling asleep beside the cart wheel.

Before the sun rose he was awake again, newly ravaged by hunger and by his first sense of coldness. He moved his head clumsily, seeking his sister, but she was far away from him, curled up in a tight ball. Instinctively he continued the search that weariness had made him forgo earlier on. He struggled forward with convulsive movements that took up much energy, the baby legs almost useless with their hardly developed muscles. He did not know why he struggled, nor why he searched. There was no fear in him now, only an insistent urge to move, to reach out. . . . It was the instinct of survival which the bitch puppy had already lost and therefore his small body was still warm and vital while hers cooled every minute closer to death.

The dog puppy managed to crawl several feet away from the shelter of the cart. He felt the different texture of the ground beneath him, rough with weeds and the crushed stubble of last year's corn. It impeded his progress and by the first sunlight he stopped in exhaustion, his trembling short limbs tangled in a dry poppy plant. The wrinkled head drooped and could lift itself no more from the ground. He sneezed violently as a scouting ant tentatively peered into one nostril, but it was his last reaction to anything for a long time.

The sun grew hot on the tiny, tawny back. The dog puppy woke again, at first blissfully aware of the warmth that engulfed him. His first waking instinct was to search for his mother. It was a ravenous instinct now and he even sucked his own paws for a while. He was engaged eagerly on this futile occupation when once again came the terrible cry that had engulfed him the day before. It had lost none of its horror for him and he froze into immobility. Now the strange ground on which he lay and the sun in which he had been basking became obvious dangers to him. Where was the hardness at his back, the company of his sister, the cool darkness that he could sense without seeing, where before he had been safe?

He was too afraid to stay still. He wanted to find again the security he had lost and he began a series of frantic, scrabbling movements which, without his knowledge, took him even farther from the place he sought and drew the attention of the carrion crow to him, although before it had been unaware of his existence.

The crow flapped over his head. The puppy felt its nearness and flattened himself to the ground. The crow came down a short distance off and stared at the puppy. It did not know quite what to make of him. A craven being, capable only of attacking the weak and the near dying, the crow could not quite decide on a course of action. It was not very hungry, having gorged the previous day, but any moving object was irresistible.

Both the crow and the puppy were still for a long time.

The puppy had no knowledge of the crow's nearness nor of its appraising watch on him. He stayed still out of fright, but, when everything was silent again and he could sense no movement, his instinct was to seek his only known safety, and again he began his ungainly struggle in search of the nest his mother had prepared for him.

The crow drew closer, head cocked, eyes and plumage gleaming. It came up behind the puppy and then drew level with him, still a short distance away but gathering the courage to attack with every passing second. It stretched its wings and began to jump about excitedly, and the puppy, suddenly aware of it again, cringed and whimpered. Instinct informed him of the danger. The unseen presence that stalked beside him, close, eager, no longer wary, filled him with helpless dread. All courage was gone. He just cringed and whimpered for his mother, sheer terror claiming him.

Pain – the first pain he had experienced – came with the sweeping downward stroke of the crow's beak. It stabbed into his ribs, just behind the shoulder. The puppy howled and was stung to movement. He tried to scrabble backwards, thin tail flattened between the haunches, and the stabbing pain came a second time, in his head. He felt the hot gushing of his own blood and began to whimper again, no longer even trying to escape.

With one more blow the crow would destroy him, but the third blow did not come. Quiveringly expecting it, the puppy was bewildered by the sudden rush of air over his head as the crow flapped madly away, screeching rage before fading from his hearing. But still the puppy cringed, sensing the closeness of another being. He still expected the death blow and was not reassured when he felt himself being grasped and pulled away from the ground. No blow came, nor any pain beyond that already inflicted, but it was frightening to be held almost upside down, a long way from the solid ground which was all he knew, caught in the embrace of some obviously all-powerful being whose intentions he could not imagine.

After the decidedly vicious actions of the crow, the first gentle administrations of a human being were something beyond the understanding of any three-day-old orphaned puppy.

2

The boy looked down at the bleeding dog puppy with curiosity. He realized that he had come upon the scene just in time to save the tiny creature's life and it was only a curiosity lingering over from the day before that had brought him to the vicinity of the farm-cart in the first place. He had heard and seen the crows, knew that they signified death or the closeness of it, and decided to investigate.

And now he held the small wounded creature in his hands and wondered. A still blind puppy was a newborn creature almost, helpless, unable to eat alone. It would be a waste of time to take it home and try to rear it. It was far too small and would surely die. It looked more than half dead already with the two huge gashes from which blood continued to stream. The boy was tempted to throw it down and leave it to the crows and then compassion stirred him and he knew he wanted to save it. It would be an achievement to rear such a creature. His mind was already racing ahead with the problems involved. It was not really worth the trouble and yet . . . .

The boy, Hilario, with dreams of becoming a doctor, knew that the puppy must be saved. It would be a proof of his ability to care for a sick creature, a life. It did not matter that the first life he saved should be that of a dog, and this dog was certainly a challenge, perhaps one of the biggest he could ever hope to be faced with. He knew nothing about dogs, had hardly ever cared for them, but the sight of wounds needing attention, the obviously encroaching death that must

be kept at bay, filled him with excitement, the zeal to tend
and save that was rarely far from him.

Even while he pondered on the small creature grasped in
his hands he could feel it growing colder. He put it back on
the ground and noticed with clinical interest that it made
no attempt to struggle away. It just lay there, defeated,
expecting death. Hilario took a large handkerchief from his
pocket, wondered for a moment what his mother would say
about his intended use for it, then spread it out on the ground
and carefully wrapped the puppy into it. It was not a wrap-
ping that satisfied him, so he unrolled the puppy again, folded
the handkerchief into a triangular shape and then rewrapped
the wilting creature, disinterested even in its own fate.

Hilario then arranged the puppy carefully within his shirt,
against his breast where it could feel warm and comfortable.
The handkerchief was already damp with blood, reminding
him of his need to treat the injuries rapidly, but he refrained
from hurrying unduly in case this might be worse for the
patient.

By the time he had reached the centre of the village,
almost home, people were beginning to stare at him. There
was a growing red patch on his shirt, a large bulge where
the puppy nestled, and the neighbours were curious. The
'patient' became just a dog again for a few minutes while
Hilario explained what he had sheltered against his breast,
and several times the puppy was pulled out, passed from hand
to hand, examined with the briefest of interest, while Hilario
watched with anxiety.

One woman remarked with a laugh, 'Your mother won't
be very pleased to see that shirt of yours, nor the handkerchief.'

'It won't live,' prophesied an old man. 'I've seen plenty
of sick animals and this is three-quarters dead already.'

He prodded the puppy about with hard, clumsy fingers.
Hilario winced and longed to snatch the injured creature

away or at least tell the man to be careful, but he knew it was his own fault for boasting of his intentions before even getting the puppy home.

At last he got it back within the shelter of his shirt and skirted anyone who might be likely to want to see what he had hidden there. The puppy stayed unmoving and soundless. Hilario worried because it seemed to have so little life. Now that he had decided to save it he was most anxious that it should not die.

3: Foster mother

Everyone advised Hilario against trying to save the life of the puppy he had found. They all agreed that it would be a waste of time. If he wanted a dog, there were plenty of healthy, older ones to choose from. He would never rear the foundling to a month's age, nor even a week's. But neither did anyone try to stop him. His mother, after scolding automatically about the stained shirt and ruined handkerchief, mixed warm milk and water in a small glass, sought a small spoon and watched with interest while he forcefully tried to feed the puppy. He was unsuccessful. The milk just dribbled from the weak jaws. The pup seemed to have lost all idea of swallowing.

He had thought feeding to be the all-important thing, but

when Hilario found this impossible, he decided to see about the curing of the wounds. This was simple enough: warm salt water and afterwards a generous soaking of iodine. The blood no longer flowed, but, though not dead, the puppy showed no particular sign of life.

'Leave him be for a while,' suggested Hilario's mother. 'Put him out in the sun. He might revive on his own.'

She found Hilario an old piece of cloth and on this he laid the limp tawny body in the warmth of the sun. He crouched beside the puppy and watched him for a long time, noticing the slightest shiver that ran through his body, or the twitch of a muscle. For a time the puppy did nothing but pant very weakly and Hilario thought, 'It won't live.'

His mother came and stood behind him for a while and once Hilario looked up at her anxiously, trying to read her thoughts. Her face was impassive, lighting up only when she saw how Hilario stared at her.

'Does it mean so much to you, the little dog?' she asked.

'Only because . . .'

He stopped, overcome by a certain shyness. What he was going to say sounded presumptuous, even to his own ears, but even as he reconsidered it he knew his mother would understand, and continued: 'Only because it's a life I should like to save.'

She ruffled her hand through his dark hair fondly and went back to the house. Hilario stayed watching the dog.

He was a tall lad of fifteen, slim and pale. His grey eyes were studious and he was pale while the rest of the lads were brown because he spent most of his time reading, writing and furiously learning. Although his father owned several fields, and his mother an orchard in another village, his parents were far from rich. They lived from year to year and could only save according to the harvests. It would never be enough to pay for their youngest child's desired career and their only hope for him was that he should win a free scholarship.

Hilario was keen to do so. He had known from an early age that doctoring was the only life that could ever interest him. He was a bright lad, quick to learn, but there were many things to study with only the schoolteacher and the priest to help him.

His parents were very proud of him. They could not quite understand how he came to be so intelligent, nor so keen to become a doctor, but they basked in the admiration and half-expressed envy of their neighbours. The village doctor encouraged him and had once half jokingly offered him the post of assistant once he should obtain his degree. Hilario took his words seriously and he dreamed only of his future, tending the sick people of his village.

He was so intent upon watching the rapidly weakening puppy that he was unaware of another person watching him.

'What have you got there?' came a voice, that of his neighbour, a stout, middle-aged man who had a kind heart beneath the gruff, unshaven exterior.

Hilario explained. The man came to look more closely but refrained from picking up the puppy.

'It won't live,' he said, 'not unless you find it another mother as soon as possible.'

'I thought of trying to feed it myself,' mentioned Hilario tentatively.

The man shook his head. 'It's too small. Were it a week or so older . . . but, look, it hasn't even opened its eyes yet. It can't be more than three or four days old. It hasn't a chance.'

He saw the disappointment in the boy's face and slapped a thick hand down on his shoulder, snorting with laughter at the same time.

'Don't worry, lad. You're in luck. If instead of always having your nose stuck in a book you used your eyes for other things you might have noticed some time or another that my own bitch is about to have puppies.'

'Truly!' exclaimed Hilario, his eyes beginning to register excitement. 'Soon?'

'Soon! If she hasn't had them already, I'll . . .'

But Hilario was already interrupting him.

'Where is she? Let's find out.'

'I expect she's somewhere in the kitchen. The wife put down a rug for her under the stairs. That's where she usually has them, you see.'

Hilario followed the neighbour into his house, exchanged a few words with the two women there, and went to look at the dog. She was where her master had expected to find her, curled up in the semi-darkness of the space under the stairs. She looked miserable and stared up at her master, whom she obviously adored, as if questioning the reason for her unhappiness. The tip of her long thin tail wavered slightly.

'You see,' said the man, 'she won't be long. As soon as she's got them you bring in the pup and we'll see if she'll foster him for you, seeing that you're set on rearing him.'

The boy felt more hopeful after this, although the puppy's weak state continued to disturb him. Several times he went to his neighbour's house to find out if the dog had whelped and each time that the answer was no he grew more anxious.

The afternoon hung on endlessly, relentlessly hot. He nursed the puppy on his lap while he sat with a Latin grammar and tried to study. But the lesson escaped him. He fondled the puppy's ears, rubbed his fingers gently over the wrinkled head, carefully avoiding the wound, and while he did so he found himself feeling a fondness for the creature, a wish for it to live beyond the purely clinical reason which had first compelled him to bring the orphaned creature home.

There had been puppies in the house before, when he was younger, but they had either died or got lost or been given away. Hilario had never felt any particular urge to own a dog. His own dreams had always been enough company for him. It was a new emotion he felt, this one of caring so personally for an animal. It was pleasant to have the tiny dog on his knees, to feel that it drew sustenance just from his company, enough at least to keep it from dying in despair. In his mind he went over the scene he had witnessed that morning and smiled down at the puppy.

He spoke to it as if it were a small child, lifting it up to the level of his face as he did so.

'As brave as a little lion you were this morning,' he told the puppy. 'And you need to be if you intend to live.'

And 'Leon' was the name he gave to it.

2

It was not until about nine o'clock that evening that Hilario's neighbour called hurriedly to tell him that the first of the puppies had been born.

'Is yours still alive?' he asked the boy. 'Bring it quickly if it is.'

Hilario, excited, rushed with the puppy to the other house.

'Give it to me,' said the man. 'I know what's the best thing to do. She'll never accept a puppy that's not hers unless we can convince her that it is.'

He spoke in a low voice. Both of them were crouched down beside the dog, watching her. She was nuzzling anxiously at the first puppy and watching them out of the corner of an eye at the same time. The presence of the boy disturbed her, but she accepted him because he was with her master. There was very little light in the kitchen, for its one window was small and the oil lamp had not yet been lighted.

Shadows enveloped the dog under the stairs. As the next puppy was born, the man took it quickly, rubbed its tiny body all over Hilario's puppy and not until the latter youngling was as damp and as in need of a licking as the first, did he suddenly push the two under the mother dog's nose.

Both watched her anxiously. She sniffed the two puppies,

one so much larger than the other, and was obviously suspicious. They both smelt of the man who had handled them; they both smelt very much alike; but she knew that something was not quite right about them and showed little eagerness to care for either of them. Again she sniffed at Leon again her nose rubbed against her own youngling. Her tongue came out in a tentative caress for the latter and she suddenly began licking more strongly pulling it closer to her to do so.

Hilario and his neighbour held their breaths. Would she pull the foundling to her also? She was a long time dealing with her own youngster and meanwhile showed no interest in the other. But then a change suddenly came over Leon. Until now he had remained inert throughout everything that was done to him. But suddenly his nose began to twitch, a slight whimper scratched in his throat, the head began to move groggily, blindly.

The mother dog stopped her licking to look at him. She stretched her muzzle to meet his and sniffed at his nostrils. The foundling puppy suddenly squirmed excitedly, again whimpering weakly and making his first efforts to draw closer to her.

'Shall we push him closer?' whispered Hilario, hardly able to bear the suspense of the moment, unable to tolerate his puppy's last-minute rejection.

'Wait,' advised his companion. 'There are times when you can't hurry an animal. It's best to leave it to her now. She'll decide.'

Even as he spoke, the dog licked out her tongue to caress the foundling puppy's injured head. The puppy squirmed again, almost painfully in his wild, unbelieving delight. He whimpered weakly, brokenly, and the bitch suddenly grasped him by the scruff of the neck and dragged him closer.

Within a moment he was nestling against her breast, burrowing his muzzle frantically into her warm body, kicking the other two puppies out of the way. There was a scuffling and a whimpering that disturbed the mother dog, unused to so much liveliness at such an early stage, and astonishment was registered in her features. She nuzzled among them, dragged them apart, but let Hilario's puppy dive down again in search of her flank.

Both the man and the boy were laughing at these antics.

'I thought you said he was lifeless,' said the bitch's master to Hilario.

'So he was. I thought it was too late already to save him.'

'Well, I've never seen such an animated corpse! He's a real cuckoo, is this dog of yours. Just look how he throws out the others! There he goes again.'

It was true. Leon had once again dislodged the other two younglings, trying to nestle against the mother body. He pushed and twisted so furiously with his blunt head that soon he had burrowed his way right under the dog's front legs and was lying with neck twisted awkwardly as he grabbed for the sustenance that he so desperately needed.

The mother dog hardly noticed these antics for the third puppy had been born and she was busily licking that in its turn. By the time she was prepared to notice Leon's behaviour, he was already flat out on his back, his tiny, hairless belly bloated, unable to move in his fullness, and blissfully unconscious.

4: Hilario

It was obvious from the beginning that Leon was going to be a big dog, much bigger than his foster brothers whom he imperiously pushed aside in his determination to be first in everything. Hilario's neighbour pointed out to the boy the largeness of the paws, the thickness of the knee joints, the breadth of the skull, the solidity of the frame.

'The mother looked a big dog,' remarked Hilario, remembering.

Leon's foster mother was a smallish animal, a mixture of all the mongrels that ran about the village, short-haired, black and tan, with a long, curly tail and particularly trusting eyes. It was obvious that she was a pet in the home of that childless couple. She was too small to warn off uninvited guests and had no thought of cringing when anyone came near her. She was naturally suspicious of Hilario at first, but when he came day after day to visit her she began to greet him with a wag of the tail and hardly minded when he picked up his own puppy to fondle.

Hilario waited anxiously for the day when the pup could be returned to his keeping. He had forgotten now that his only interest in it had been in saving its life. That life had been assured when first Leon burrowed himself under the friendly little bitch and she accepted him, and Hilario could hardly take the credit for it. Now his interest was purely that inspired by affection, the age-old stirring of man for dog, and he watched the little creature's progress with impatient attention, thrilled at the first opening of the eyes, dark blue and weak-looking, anxious for the day when those eyes would first look to him as master.

He hardly noticed the other puppies which were inferior creatures in comparison with his Leon, smaller, uglier and weaker than he who had forced himself to first place in everything. One of the litter died soon after birth, but the little bitch had enough with her own two and Leon, for the latter had the strength and persistence of five puppies rolled into one. Whether she ever realized that he was not her own offspring it was impossible to tell. She treated him as well as he demanded of her, always pushing himself under her nose for attention, and the other two were often rather neglected in comparison, thrust aside by the strong strokes of Leon's back legs.

But for all his strength he was not very adventurous, clinging to the mother dog as if afraid of losing her. As the days and weeks passed by the others began to stir from her side, making short sallies into the kitchen or grubbing about under the stairs, but Leon stayed on the rug beneath her and whimpered for her when she was gone.

By the time he was four weeks old, Hilario collected him and took him home. He had more than doubled in size in that time and was stocky as well as large, his head no longer so blunt but beginning to taper to a finer point. His general appearance promised handsomeness and strength, which pleased everyone in the family.

Hilario's father said that he should be trained as a guard dog. Someone had stolen a chicken from the yard only the night before, or perhaps it had been a dog or a bird of prey.

'Either way, we could do with a dog in the yard,' he said.

Hilario, not wishing to disagree, nor wishing to assent, for he had finer plans for his Leon, said only: 'He'll have to grow first, though. Meanwhile, can I keep him in the house?'

'Ask your mother about that, but don't bring him up with bad habits.'

Hilario's father could have no understanding of his son's ideas for the dog. A hard-working farmer who had known only struggle, long days and, when the harvests were bad, poor fare on the table, he had little time for finer sentiments. He was a man of few words, used to spending long hours alone with rarely even a mule for company and the empty countryside stretching for endless miles on every side of him.

His son knew this. He had been used to his father's few words from babyhood and knew that behind them there was much affection. But he knew that it would be a waste of time trying to express his own plans and ideas. Enough that he should say to his father, 'I want to be a doctor,' or, 'I want to keep a dog.' From then on he must let his actions speak, for these the farmer understood with clarity. So he studied hard to gain a scholarship and, in the same manner, he would treat the dog in his own way and one day his father would see the results. And, if he did not understand the intelligence of which such a dog was capable, at least Hilario would make him realize that Leon was not a dog to be tied all day long in the patio, looking out for robbers that would probably never come.

Even had Hilario's father asked the boy to formulate his ideas for the dog, at this point he could not have done so. They were mostly dreams. He only knew instinctively that Leon was to be a special dog, his particular companion, and that an association could be built up between them difficult to explain with words.

But when Leon was only four weeks old, and Hilario really had him in his definite possession for the first time, a strong, healthy, wriggling puppy, he had no time for the exalted ideas which were to come later. He was just like any other boy with his first dog, whether five years of age or fifteen, delighted with everything about him. There was something strangely satisfying about being able to hold a living creature in his arms and tell himself, 'He's mine, he's mine.'

2

For Leon there was nothing delightful about the occasion. For the second time he had lost his mother and all that concerned him was the lack of her and the strangeness of the house to which he had been brought.

It was just as well that Hilario did not speak to his father of the dog's intelligence, for on that first day there was nothing to suggest anything but the dimmest of understanding in the animal brain. Leon stood stolidly and dumbly where Hilario had placed him, in the middle of the kitchen floor, neither anxious to explore, nor play, nor seek friendship with someone. He ignored the snapping fingers, the vain calling of his name over and over again, the clicking tongues and whistles. He just stared into space with who can imagine what cataclasm of feelings; torn from the little bitch that had nursed him until an hour previously, placed in a strange home whose smells he knew not, hearing voices which previously he had never heard, except for Hilario's to which he had never paid heed.

'Perhaps we should give him something,' suggested Hilario's mother. In her view the dog's behaviour was strange.

'Some milk,' suggested Hilario.

'Milk! That's a fine way to start his life with us. Milk for a dog!'

She grumbled for another five minutes, but at the same time was drawing milk from the pitcher in the larder and pouring a small quantity into an old cracked plate.

The milk was put on the floor under the puppy's nose. Leon showed fear of the plate and backed away. Hilario bent to put him beside the plate again and forced the little head down to sniff at it. Leon began to struggle.

'I don't think he's hungry yet,' said Hilario. 'I'll give it to him later.'

The three humans towered above the dog and Leon cringed beneath their gaze. He began to whimper softly and then he made a puddle on the floor.

Hilario's father said: 'You should keep him out in the patio. Dogs don't belong in houses.'

The boy took the dog in his arms. He had been wanting to do so for the last five minutes but his father's uncompassionate gaze upon the little creature had withheld him.

'I'll take him outside for a while,' he said, glad to escape with Leon.

He stood just outside the kitchen door, fondling the dog's ears. The summer moon was a silver crescent in the still pale sky and it was too early for stars. The sun had not yet set, although shadows were heavy in the village and the swallows were flying homewards, almost touching the ground with their dark bodies, bat-like in movement.

He could hear his father say, 'What does he want with a dog at his age? Surely he has enough with his studies without having to bother with a dog?'

His mother answered, 'It's something to amuse him, that's all. He can't be studying all the time. He's only a boy after all.'

'What is there to eat?' said his father next. As far as he was concerned, the subject of the dog was finished.

Hilario smiled listening to them. He smiled because he had Leon in his arms, because the falling dusk was cool and pleasant, because his parents were so reliable in their unfailing acceptance of everything he did or wanted. Even as he smiled, Leon suddenly reached up and licked his nose.

He felt comfortable in the boy's grasp: warm and safe. It was the nearest thing he could find to his lost foster mother. When Hilario put him to the ground to snuffle about in the straw he began to whimper again.

'Silly,' admonished Hilario softly.

He was still shy about talking affectionately to the puppy and did not want his father to overhear. He was not accustomed to talking to an animal, but he supposed that it would be the same as talking to a small child.

'Silly,' he reiterated as the puppy continued to whimper. 'Didn't I call you Leon because once you were valiant? Are you a coward after all?'

He knelt down and scratched the puppy's head, feeling with his finger the indented scar that remained to tell how deeply the crow had pecked him. Leon stopped whimpering and drew nearer to the boy. He would have been quite happy like this, for a minute not remembering his foster mother, for he was not hungry, but Hilario was called in to the meal and the fondling stopped.

'Let's go,' he said to the puppy, hoping to animate him a little, and Leon, watching the legs that were rapidly moving away, followed with bounding, clumsy leaps, afraid to lose them. Hilario grinned and encouraged him with snapping fingers and while he sat at the table to eat the puppy stretched himself across his sandalled feet, licking his ankles.

That evening, after a clumsy effort or so, Leon learned to lap up the milk from the plate. He refused the remains of the meal that were put down for him and looked rather doleful when he realized that there was no more milk. Hilario's mother, at her son's request, found a piece of sacking that would do for the dog's bed and the boy tried to make Leon comfortable under the stairs.

Then everyone went to bed and the oil lamp was put out. Leon was alone in the kitchen. At first he was tired and dozed for a while, but by the time voices and footsteps had faded and the house was in darkness, evaded by the night's still-ness which was broken only by the rustlings of mice or cockroaches, the puppy was very much awake and very much afraid.

He remembered that Hilario had gone up the stairs and decided to look for him, but the stone steps were too steep and their dark prospect discouraging. He began to whimper and the sound of his unhappiness was loud in his own ears. No one seemed to hear him and every minute the kitchen was larger, darker and more lonely. He longed for the little bitch that had nursed him, the foster brothers with whom he had quarrelled and played, the boy who had befriended him, and such unhappiness welled within him that soon it overflowed into the most doleful whine of which he was capable.

This new sound that he had made upset him still more and the cries began to pour out of him. He put his whole soul into them. His stocky frame heaved with mournful howls which, within seconds, had grown from nothing into a crescendo.

A heavy voice cursed him. A lighter voice followed, but equally stern, and Leon wept even louder, unable to stop now and frightening himself. Then there was a third voice, and a sound of movement on the stairs. It was a whispering voice, the one he had been waiting for, and the howls subsided into tiny yelps of gratified pleasure.

He slobbered all over Hilario's face and hands, almost breaking himself in two as his tail wagged wildly.

'Keep that dog silent!' called Hilario's father fiercely.

'Sssh!' breathed the boy, gathering Leon still wriggling and excited into his arms. He took him up the stairs to his bedroom, which was flooded with moonlight, and dropped him down on to the bed.

Leon wanted to play. He jumped up and down, slobbering, galloping over the crumpled sheets, and it took all Hilario's efforts to restrain him. He did so finally by lying down himself and drawing the puppy closely to him, stroking him gently over and over again and whispering his name.

The puppy calmed himself, weary with howling and the overflowing of excitement. He nuzzled close to the boy's bare chest and closed his eyes with a deep sigh of contentment.

Hilario continued to stroke him, mumbling his name. Soon afterwards, when the puppy was breathing evenly, the boy was silent and his fingers fell away. The moon watched over them both.

5: Learning

It did not take Hilario long to lose his heart to the dog, nor for the dog to lose his heart to Hilario in return. From the very beginning Leon slept at night on the boy's bed and nothing was said by Hilario's parents although they did not approve. The farmer had never heard of a dog sleeping on a person's bed and his wife worried about fleas. But as Hilario was their only son, as well as being the youngest in the family and with so bright a career ahead of him, he could do no wrong in their eyes and was allowed to do as he wished.

The first morning that Hilario went off to his studies in the priest's house without Leon the puppy howled so woefully, tied out in the patio by the mother, that in future the boy always took the dog with him. Leon was a nuisance at first, wanting constantly to play and be noticed, but the priest was a patient man, fond of animals, and he had no objection to the puppy sharing the Greek and Latin lessons.

Soon the puppy learned that he must lie still at his master's feet. He learned this out of sheer boredom, for, after the first couple of mornings, neither the boy nor the priest paid any heed to him and the room was too barren to be interesting. So he curled across Hilario's sandals and licked the dusty feet, gratified to feel the boy's toes gently scratching him from time to time, although no word was said.

From going to the priest's house, he began to follow Hilario to the classroom and to the teacher's house also. Hilario was older than all the other children in the school, for none stayed beyond their fourteenth year and many of them had left by the age of eleven or twelve. He therefore studied alone, advanced mathematics, the Spanish language, history, geography, all the required syllabus for the hopeful candidate for a scholarship. Sometimes the puppy slept on Hilario's lap, but mostly he was at his feet, learning patience early in life, for when Hilario was studying the puppy was forgotten.

But the boy was not always studying. When the morning and evening lessons were over, then would come the happiest time for the dog. Stopping only to leave his books in the house, Hilario would be off across the fields with Leon, the latter barking wildly, romping from side to side, ever impatient of his master's slow pace, although, in the early days, he was generally so tired on the homeward journey that Hilario often had to carry him.

It was when they were alone together beyond the outskirts of the village, perhaps having stopped in the shade of a solitary pine tree, that Hilario would show the most affection to his dog, talking to him, fondling him, teaching him to obey simple commands.

Hilario was shy of being openly affectionate with the dog at home. His father would watch him sceptically, wondering if his only son were a bit queer in the head, and his mother would scoff and say that the dog was a nuisance, always dirtying the house. Therefore he saved his demonstrations of affection for when they were alone.

He would fondle Leon lengthily to make up for all the hours of ignoring him; talk to him as if he were a small child; teach him to sit, to come and to go at a word, to fetch and to beg. These simple accomplishments seemed ample enough in Hilario's eyes. There were few dogs in the village capable of so much. But he knew that Leon had great capabilities, an intelligence not yet developed but which one day must be employed.

He had read of dogs in Switzerland that searched for men lost in the snow; he had read of the wonderful intelligence of the German shepherd dogs and of the way some dogs were trained to guide the blind. Surely his Leon, intelligent and brave, could be taught to do something?

He watched the puppy's growth with unflagging interest and took pleasure in talking to him, for although Leon was incapable of voicing words, he had his own way of communicating with the boy, which was with his ears and his eyes and the contortions of his body. While very young, it was mostly the latter that spoke for him, telling Hilario that the puppy was generally wildly enthusiastic about life. The stocky long body would wriggle and twist into the most incredible shapes just at a word from Hilario or at the touch of his hand.

When Hilario was reading somewhere out in the country, his shoulders pillowed against a bank of earth and the dog lying not far from his side, he would occasionally remember to look up from the page to Leon and always the dog would be watching him. Sometimes the boy would say nothing, just stare at the dog with affection. The dog would stare back, the blue-black eyes eager, expectant, watching the boy's lips for the first word that would spring to them. He was waiting for 'Leon', the sound that made him belong to Hilario, the first sound of love between them. If the boy refused to speak Leon would grow impatient, a soft whine starting in his throat, and then if Hilario stretched out his hand he would jump up with a yelp of delight, squirming and silly, slobbering all over the boy's face and pushing the book away.

Hilario would rescue the book with a cry, command the dog to lie down again, and Leon would do so, gazing upon his master with such mournful, contrite expression that in the end the boy would say, 'Leon, don't look at me like that. You already know that I love you.'

And at this sign of weakness on the boy's part Leon would be up and squirming again, as ridiculously happy as only a dog can be.

Sometimes Hilario liked to tease him. He would move his lips as if about to give some command and Leon would watch him, eyes brilliant, ears pricked, whole body quivering, half raised from the ground. This would go on for several seconds, the dog at the ready, until Hilario would collapse into laughter and Leon would jump on top of him, clumsy paws scratching, tongue dripping, tail wagging wildly.

But when the boy and the dog came home Leon would follow at his master's heels, hardly lifting his nose from the level of Hilario's ankle, and no one would ever guess to look at them that, alone in the countryside, they wrestled together and laughed, the boy with his voice and the dog with his eyes.

Leon had learned that when Hilario's father was at home it was best for him to be out of the way, on his rug under the stairs where, when the meal was over, he would be given a plateful of beans or rice or chick peas, whatever happened to be left over that day.

As a small puppy he had very much objected to the fare that was put down for him, preferring hunger to the unchanging, stodgy diet. He wanted milk and he wanted meat. While he was very small, Hilario's mother allowed him a plateful of milk each morning, but that was soon curtailed as milk was for people, not dogs. The only meat that ever came his way was that which remained on the chicken or rabbit bones, already well cleaned when they reached him. At the beginning he nearly choked over the bones, ravening at the first taste of meat – although taste was almost all it ever was – but he learned to save the bones until the worst of his hunger was satisfied, when he would settle down to crack them with less haste.

It was his quest for meat that first encouraged him to chase the chickens in the yard and taught him to respect Hilario's father, if not to fear him. He was having great fun, scattering them in all directions, unafraid of their squawks, their flapping wings and flying feathers. It was lunchtime and Hilario's chair was farthest from the door, so that, before he had time to jump up and curtail the puppy's adventure, his father was already at the door.

The farmer grabbed a broom and as the puppy came dashing by, unaware of anything but the bliss of having all these fat birds afraid of him and flying before him, brought it down with a whack across Leon's back. The excited barks changed in the instant to yelps of surprise, fear and pain. Leon fled with his tail between his legs and it was hours before he returned.

Hilario pretended nonchalance, but he could not disguise from his mother how worried he was by his dog's disappearance. He pretended to read in the kitchen, but his eyes kept straying to the door. In the end she said, 'Don't worry. He'll be back. He knows where he's fed.'

Leon did come, returning unsure and cringing. Until now no one had ever hurt him and the world he knew had come apart with the intentional blow that had almost cracked his ribs. Hilario was about to gather him in his arms and make a fuss of him, but for once his mother interfered.

'Leave him,' she said, 'or put him in his place under the

stairs. He must learn to leave the chickens alone and he won't do so if you spoil him.'

Hilario did as he was bade, but was as sulky as the dog for a while until he could see the sense of his mother's words. By the time the farmer had returned home in the evening, Leon had been forgiven, but ever after that he learned to be very circumspect in the man's presence.

The sound of his approaching feet would send him flying to his corner, and while he was in the house Leon either stayed under the stairs or kept very close to Hilario. He never chased the chickens again and with time learned to find his own meat in the form of insects or mice and rats.

Sometimes Hilario's father would bring home a hare that he had caught in the fields and Leon's share would be the innards, the skin and the ears. As a small puppy, it was hard work chewing his way through the fur-thick hide and sometimes he would have it for days, worrying it, growling and pouncing on it, rarely even trying to eat it. But by the time he had reached full size, bigger than his mother and the wolf dog that had sired him, he would wait with drooling jaws for the skin to be flung in his direction, swallowing it in hardly more than one gulp.

2

There was only one man in the district who owned a pure-blooded German shepherd dog, or wolf dog as they are called in Spain, and he was the rich man who owned three-quarters of the wheatlands that surrounded the village. One of his sons had spent a year in Germany studying engineering and on his return had brought his father a black and tan wolf dog to guard the immediate vicinity of the house.

Everyone in the village admired the dog. It could be seen now and again outside the tavern, when his master came for a drink, or outside the church on a Sunday morning. No one dared approach it, although it had never shown itself particu-

larly ferocious, but it was so large, so beautiful, and so power-
ful in appearance that it was always admired from a distance
and gazed upon with respect.

By the time Leon was six months old there was no doubt
in the minds of any of the villagers that, for all the mongrel
breeding on his mother's side, none other than the German
wolf dog could be his sire. The pricked triangular ears –
which lost their shape because Hilario was always fondling
them; the long, solid nose and shape of the head. Everything
in the dog's form pointed to the wolf dog as his sire, even
though his colouring followed that of the mongrel mother,
a deep tawny shade, intermingled with only a few darker
hairs in the thick shoulders and feathery tail.

Leon's hair was longer than his sire's and when he was
lying down, but with his head held high, he really looked
like the beast that was his namesake, for the ruff round his
neck was like a mane over his strong muscles and his gaze was
always noble and serene, bright with intelligence.

There was no proof of the dog's parentage, except that
everyone remarked on the likeness and was sure that no other
dog could have sired such a one as Leon. The best proof came
when the owner of the wolf dog approached Hilario's father
and offered to buy Leon.

'What do you want for him?' he asked one Sunday morning when the church service was over. He spoke to the
farmer although he knew that the dog belonged to Hilario.

The farmer hesitated. He had a natural respect for the man
who spoke to him and was even embarrassed to be the centre
of attention. He felt proud, too, to know that in his house was
something that the rich man desired, and all these unusual
feelings made him tongue-tied. He could feel his son's anxiety,
for the boy was behind him with the dog at his heels, and at
last found words enough to say, 'I'm sorry, Don Agustín,
but the dog isn't mine to sell. You must ask my son who
found him and saved his life.'

The rich man looked at Hilario and recognized him.

'You're the lad who wants to be a doctor, no? A worthy sentiment and I hope you succeed. Now tell me, what do you want for the dog? I appreciate all that you've done for him and that it must have cost a lot to rear him. A dog of his size eats a great deal.'

'He's not for sale,' said Hilario quietly.

Don Agustín laughed at the boy's serious face.

'What do you want with a dog like that? Surely you can see that he's far more useful to me? I have large properties that need to be watched over and a second dog would be useful to me. How much do you want?'

'Nothing,' said Hilario adamantly.

He knew that he was annoying his parents by his stubbornness but refused to be intimidated by the other's wealth.

'Come now,' replied Don Agustín jovially, all the more determined to possess the dog. 'You'll want friends when you go to the hospital school. I can help you find them.'

'I haven't yet won the scholarship,' contested Hilario, growing hotly angry at the man's arrogance.

Everyone was watching the scene which from a condescending conversation had become a battle of wills. Don Agustín became aware of the crowd that had gathered and lost his temper. That this pale-faced farmer's lad should defy him was beyond his comprehension.

'Instead of teaching you Latin they should teach you some respect!' he cried, and turned away.

The people made way for him, but continued to stare as he climbed into the car in which his family was already seated, together with the dog. It was about the only car that ever entered the village, and Hilario, together with all the other lads, had often admired it.

When it had gone, lost in a cloud of dust kicked up by the wheels, Hilario's mother turned angrily to her son.

'You're a fool,' she cried, 'to annoy Don Agustín, and all

for the sake of a dog! The money would have been useful and it's not every day that it's offered to one.'

The villagers agreed with her. They had begun to envy Hilario his opportunity and, like his mother, could not comprehend his refusing any money that Don Agustín might offer him.

The boy said nothing, red in the face and sullen. His sister was there with her husband and her baby. She joined in. 'You've always let my brother go his own way and this is what you get for it. Refusing good money from Don Agustín and annoying him into the bargain. He won't win the scholarship now, you'll see.'

At this moment the farmer suddenly came to his son's defence.

'Silence,' he commanded gruffly. 'So much fuss over a dog. Don Agustín can afford to get another dog from Germany if he wishes. Why should he try to deprive my son of his dog?' And to his wife, 'Let's go home.'

With these words he dragged his family home and forbade his wife to mention the subject again. Hilario was grateful to him, for without his backing he knew he would have had to surrender Leon. He had not the strength to defy Don Agustín alone.

6: The shepherd

It was not until Leon was more than a year old that Hilario had the opportunity of really appreciating the dog's intelligence and understanding. Hilario's eldest sister had married a shepherd and lived in a village some fifteen miles away. As it was too distant for the two families to keep in frequent touch, Hilario grew into the habit of spending two or three weeks with them during the winter months and a month or more in the summer.

Because of the narrow, unchanging life that he led in his own village this was almost a big adventure. His brother-in-law's village was hardly any larger and the people were much the same, neither rich nor poor, but away from his home Hilario had more freedom and the people appeared to be more interesting. His brother-in-law treated him as a man and his sister spoiled him, pleased to have someone who could bring her news of her home and parents.

They both made a lot of fuss of Leon even though the first time Hilario went with the dog was disastrous. Still very much a puppy, he dashed and gambolled everywhere and his large, clumsy frame made him responsible for many accidents. He terrified the two little boys of the house, suddenly confronted by gaping jaws, shining teeth and a huge tongue that slobbered over their small faces; or big paws suddenly upon their shoulders, knocking them over.

Hilario spent much of his day with his brother-in-law, Nicolás, watching the sheep in the fields. Nicolás had a small dog of his own, a little bitch that immediately took umbrage at the presence of the large, idiot puppy that frolicked at Hilario's side. She flew at Leon and sent him yelping away, tail between his legs, although she was hardly half his size. She resented his presence anywhere near her master's sheep and with good reason, for one day Leon accidentally got among them and caused havoc.

Much as he had done with the chickens, he set them galloping in all directions. Luckily, Nicolás was a young man with a sense of humour. He laughed so much that for a long time he could not even think of gathering the flock together again. Then he sent the little mongrel off with a few sharp words and within half an hour the ewes were once again a flock and none were missing.

When Hilario saw the cleverness of the little bitch he was greatly chagrined by his own dog's behaviour. Leon had disappeared after realizing that he had behaved very badly and hours passed before he came cringing back to his master, no doubt recalling the incident of the chickens. Hilario was loath to punish him. He had never touched his dog in real anger and had only ever chided him gently, but the memory of the cleverness of the shepherd's dog deeply injured his pride and faith in Leon.

Earlier he had been teasing Leon with a long twig that he had found by the wayside. Now with the same stick he thrashed him and sent the dog howling away again. Nicolás and the little mongrel watched in silence.

Afterwards the shepherd said, 'He's only a young dog. You should make allowances for him. He's not used to sheep yet. You shouldn't have punished him.'

Hilario sat on a mound with his back to the man, staring at the still nervous sheep. He made no answer. He could make none, for he was trying hard not to cry.

The second time that Hilario went to stay with his sister and Nicolás, Leon behaved very circumspectly. He was so quiet, hardly moving from the boy's side in the house nor from his call in the country, that even the shepherd's dog began to realize that perhaps he was improving and decided to strike up a condescending acquaintanceship with him. This was in the winter. Leon had grown a thick, bear-like coat and was larger still and very handsome. Nicolás would have liked to own him and his little mongrel grew quite jealous of the looks her master directed at the idiot puppy that had come to stay in the house again.

There was solid snow on the ground, more than three feet deep in places, and Nicolás kept his flock corralled near the house. Every day he and Hilario took food to them. Sometimes it was not very much nor very good in quality. It was a busy time of year for the shepherd, with newborn lambs to be kept safe from cold and from hawks, and the mothers to be kept from hunger.

Leon continued to follow his master wherever he went and soon he began to show a more formal interest in the sheep, watching them with pricked ears and alert eyes while his master and the other man worked, often with the company of the shepherd's mongrel beside him. He learned deportment from the sagacious creature; that it was wrong to bark and gambol within close vicinity of the silly, woolly animals; that movements among them must be determined, precise and very cautious, so easily were they frightened.

By the time the summer had come round again and Hilario brought him for the third time to the shepherd's village, Leon was more than a year old and his intelligence was rapidly developing. Hilario was aware of Leon's increasing maturity. It could be seen in the way the dog watched and studied everything, from the smallest grasshopper injured on the ground, unable to escape his gaze, to the shodding of a mule by the village blacksmith. The dog really observed life, and Hilario, a still much greater observer, was excited by the prospect of his dog's intelligence.

It was easy for him to talk to Nicolás about his dog's prospects, for the shepherd had spent a lifetime with animals and had much sympathy for them. He agreed with the boy's insistence that Leon could be taught almost anything, but up to now there had really been nothing to teach him beyond a few tricks and simple commands.

It was the dog himself that showed his master and Nicolás of what he was capable. They had noticed the eagerness with which he continuously watched the shepherd's flock and when one morning he suddenly got up from his place at Hilario's side and began loping down the slope towards it, they both stared expectantly, wondering what he would do. Nicolás's mongrel had jumped to all fours, growling, but the shepherd held her back with a sharp command and she sank down again, though continuing to growl.

Then Nicolás and Hilario noticed what had earlier slipped their combined gaze and that only Leon had seen. One of the ewes had separated from the flock and was grazing at quite a distance from it, gradually wandering farther and farther away in her search for something to pull at. Both watched with intense interest and Hilario could hardly breathe in his strained excitement, for Leon was demonstrating a knowledge of sheep that no one, not even the little bitch, could have taught him; an instinctive understanding that must have come to him through his paternal ancestors in far-away Germany.

Circling round the ewe, he managed to remain unseen by her until he was fairly close, when he suddenly dropped down and began to creep up on her, so insidiously that although his movements at last caught her attention they did not startle her unduly. She stared at the now still dog, jaws munching rapidly, then dropped her head to graze again.

Leon wriggled a little closer. Again she stared, slightly disturbed by him. She suddenly looked round for the rest of the flock, found it a long way off and panicked. With a loud bleat, she broke into a canter and then Leon was up and loping behind her, heading her in a straight line to her companions, allowing her no opportunity to escape again. As soon as she reached the nearest ewe he left her.

He stared at the flock and circled round it at a wide distance, pushing a few of the stragglers closer and, when satisfied with the general position, came loping back up the hill to his master, tongue lolling and eyes gleaming. Hilario received him with open arms which he flung round the dog's neck, enthusiastic with praise which never came shyly in the presence of Nicolás. Before Leon would have been crumpled on the ground in delight, kicking his legs in the air like a puppy, but it seemed that now he had suddenly grown a sense of dignity, for he accepted Hilario's praise as just reward, wagged his tail with swaying haunches, gave him only one lick on the nose, then flopped down to resume his watch over the sheep, ignoring his master.

After that Hilario and the shepherd encouraged him daily to care for the sheep. They allowed him full rein and it was difficult to believe how restrained the dog could become, his whole body tightened to the movement of a mere centimetre at a time, stalking a tough old ram that would crush his ribs with one blow if angered enough; the gentle herding of a lost lamb, pushing it along with his muzzle until the mother would come bleating to retrieve it; the endless patience with which he persuaded a dim-brained ewe to behave itself.

Leon had a sure instinct, a natural gentleness combined with an ability to dominate which was the marvel of the shepherd and Hilario and every other man in the village who came to watch him. Even the little mongrel no longer despised him, although her jealousy grew.

2

It was with regret that Hilario had to return home after his stay in his sister's house. For the first time he could really boast of his dog's prowess and it was pleasant to have people in the village wanting to talk to him about Leon and even offer to buy him. Before he set out on the morning of his long walk home, Nicolás said to him with certain wistfulness, but not much hope, 'I suppose you wouldn't like to leave the dog with me? It's obvious that he's devoted to this skill of his and it's a pity not to use it.'

Hilario shook his head. 'I'm sorry but . . . you understand.'

Nicolás slapped him on the shoulder and told him not to think about it.

'But make that dog work,' were his last words of advice. 'He's too intelligent to be left to idleness.'

That day the fifteen miles seemed shorter than they had ever been. Hilario was bursting to reach home with his great news and at times ran like a boy, Leon loping beside him. He stopped to share his bread and lamb chops with the dog, at first only throwing Leon the bones which he cracked with a pained expression. Hilario's sister had been generous with the last meal she would prepare him until winter came and, in his overflowing pride and joy in his dog, Hilario gave Leon two whole chops for himself, those with the most meat. He could imagine his mother's scandalized voice but did not care. She could not see him and would never know and a dog of Leon's magnificence deserved meat now and again. It was not very much after all.

Hilario told his father of Leon's cleverness, but the farmer was not very impressed. He knew little of sheep, for this was a community of arable farmers and the only animals he knew were the oxen he hired to pull his plough without understanding much about them. His mother was pleased with the success the dog had brought him in the other village and soon the news was known to everyone, spread by her when she went down to wash the clothes among the other women.

For a week or two Hilario basked in the glory of his dog, but when he was back into his usual routine, with even more things to be learned for the examination that loomed nearer, and Leon seemed to have reverted to a dog that did nothing but mooch at his feet while he studied, the wonder of it faded and became just a dream.

But the bond between the dog and the boy grew stronger. By this time Leon had stopped following Hilario to the house of the priest or the schoolmaster. He had learned that there were times when the boy must go off alone and, although he had accepted this, he was never happy by himself. He would wait outside the kitchen door for Hilario's return, eyes doleful, muzzle resting on his paws. He was never a dog to go wandering about the village on his own, ever dependent upon his master's will and living only to accomplish it.

His most miserable moments were when Hilario told him to stay and walked off without him. He obeyed because it was expected of him, but he made the boy feel guilty by the forsaken expression that immediately overtook him, the sad eyes, the flattened ears, the drooping tail.

Sometimes he would perform this act so well that Hilario would burst into laughter and scold, 'Go on, you good-for-nothing. It's not the end of the world!' and Leon would be very hurt by his derision, the ultimate dejection.

One day the farmer said, 'That dog has a better life than I do. No work, food dished up twice a day and so much attention that he might be a king. What will he do when you've gone to that hospital so far away and there's no one to come drooling over him?'

Hilario was silent. He had not thought of this before. Going to the hospital was still almost a dream. He had to be at least eighteen and first of all pass the examination.

At last he said, 'If I go, I shall leave him with Nicolás. He'll look after him for me.'

But for the first time the thought of going so far from home disturbed him and the great adventure palled a little. Leon was the most tangible thing in his world for the present and the rest was a hardly visible glimmer on a distant horizon.

7: Rich man's offer

Although Hilario had few companions he was not a lonely boy. His studies filled up much of his time and when he was free of them most often he wanted to wander about the countryside, his brain needing to unwind slowly from the long hours with his books. A human companion would have molested him. He wanted to think of nothing. He wanted only to feel the wind tugging at his shirt and hair, fresh in his face, and see the changes in the landscape on every side of him. In this Leon was his best companion. Having the dog, he was not alone. He did not need to talk to him, just a touch of his fingers was enough, and if he wished to be silent he could be so without being considered surly by his companion.

But there were days when he wanted company of his own kind. On the light evenings he would sometimes go hunting with the other lads, armed with catapults or sticks and stones, and they would stir up a hare from its form, aided by the dogs that followed with as much excitement. Leon loved this sport and as he was the swiftest among the mongrels he would often provide a thrilling spectacle for the lads, racing his heart out

in an effort to catch the bulging-eyed hare but never suc-
ceeding.

After a while he would change tactics and try to herd the
hare back in the direction of the boys, when they would pelt it
with stones, rarely touching the swift, zig-zagging target.
Mostly the hare made his escape. If he were caught his hunters
would rush about to gather fuel enough for a small fire; a few
sharp sticks would be found for skewering the various pieces
and it would be eaten half cooked and saltless with the greatest
of pleasure while the dogs squabbled over the skin, the entrails
and the bones.

On summer nights, by the light of a full or semi-full moon,
they would seek a different prey under the banks of the stream:
the small fresh-water lobster – crayfish – that had to be grasped
with care and skill. Only dogs capable of keeping silent were
allowed to join this expedition and Leon was among them,
unable to share the emotion of the hunters but watching with
comical expression his moonlit reflection in the rippling
water, capering about on expeditions of his own, soon bored
by the intense behaviour of the humans. He much preferred
the chase.

Later, if enough crayfish were caught to make it worth
while, a fire would be lit to bake them and then Leon would
draw close and lie on the ground beside his master, staring at
the flickering flames as if hypnotized. He would continue to
stare, long after they had died into a glow of hot ashes, his
nose stretched out on his paws, his eyes narrowed, almost
asleep and feeling at peace with the world. He would feel
Hilario's hand scratching slowly round his neck, under his
chin, and he would let fall a sigh of contentment. He expected
nothing more of life than this.

But the time passed rapidly. Between the changing of the
seasons, the pleasures of visiting the friendly house of the
shepherd, the excitement of chases and fishing expeditions, the
hungry anticipation of the annual pig-stickings, and all the

many small things that went to make up the almost uneventful year of that little community, Leon became a dog in his prime and Hilario almost a man.

In the December of 1935 Hilario and Leon had their first taste of separation from each other when the former, intense with emotion and pale of face, made the long journey to the nearest big town to sit for the long-awaited examination. He was to be away from home for four days, two days for travelling and two for the examination.

Hilario watched his mother pack a small suitcase with care. It was not that there was much to pack, Hilario had only one decent suit and two shirts, but she was very much determined that he should make a good impression by his appearance at least. She spent almost half an hour polishing his black shoes until she could see her face in them and when Leon took a glimpse also, with hot breath and lolling tongue, she whacked him on the skull with the shoe-brush because he spoiled the shine. After that he drew back to a safe distance to watch her, as interested as Hilario though not yet understanding the meaning of it all.

After a second polish the shoes were wrapped in newspaper and in another sheet Hilario's mother put the brush and the polish so that her son could clean them again on removing them from the case. His suit was carefully pressed with a relay of three irons heating on the stove, and this she folded into a scrap of sheeting to preserve the proper creases and prevent others. His best shirt was folded carefully and laid on top together with the blue tie that he only wore to church, two white handkerchiefs and a pair of socks.

Leon only understood when early on the morning of his departure Hilario put a strong cord round his neck and tied him to the wall in the yard. He tied up the dog because he was afraid that Leon would follow and he talked to him coaxingly, hoping he would understand. Leon saw him walk out of the house with the suitcase, a parent on either side of him, and even though he barked excitedly, Hilario refused to turn his head. In this manner the dog understood that his master was going away and he dragged against the cord, barking and yelping, until his throat was dry and his neck ached. Then he flopped down, panting hard, distressed because he knew the futility of his efforts.

Later on the farmer and his wife came back alone. They hardly noticed the dog, thinking only of the son setting out on his first long journey alone.

After dinner the woman brought Leon his usual plateful of left-overs, but she said nothing to him and the dog did not even rise from where he lay. Throughout the whole afternoon, short because the sun was gone by half past four, he moved only to find a sunny spot, and after the evening meal the woman did not bring him any food because she had noticed that he had eaten nothing. It was bitterly cold, so she brought him into the kitchen as he looked so dejected, but Leon did not sleep. He spent the night prowling about the house restlessly, knowing that Hilario was not sleeping in his room above.

He passed all the four days of Hilario's absence thus, tied out in the yard during the day and lonely in the house at night, without eating and hardly sleeping. He spent the daytime watching the direction in which Hilario had gone and the night-time watching the door through which he would come.

When Hilario did return he went wild with excitement, whimpering like a beaten puppy at first, then almost knocking the lad over in his attempts to lick his face. Hilario was as gay as his dog and covered him with caresses, regardless of his watching parents.

His father said, 'It looks as though it pleases you more to see the dog than to see your parents,' but Hilario only laughed at the gentle rebuke and went to hug them both.

He refused to talk about his experiences until he had unpacked his suitcase and brought out the various presents he had purchased in Valladolid with money supplied by relations. There was a bottle of eau-de-Cologne for his mother, tobacco for his father and similar objects for other members of the family who were to be invited to the house that evening to celebrate his return.

Only when the excitement of his homecoming had died down, when Leon was calm at his feet, and his parents were considering him seriously across the table and the meal was over, did he say, 'The exam was easier than I expected. I'm sure I've passed.'

His mother burst into tears, his father looked gravely pleased and everyone was very happy, including Leon, who could not know that Hilario's success would mean the end of their association.

2

One morning, a month or so later, a message came from Don Agustín asking Hilario to go and see him, taking the dog. The whole family was puzzled and Hilario was particularly perturbed by the second request as, at four in the afternoon, he set out with Leon to walk the three miles to the rich man's house. It was already dark and the ground was snowy. Hilario was glad to have his dog for company, for it was a lonely road at dusk and the small lantern he carried seemed to emphasize the gloom about him instead of dispelling it.

Don Agustín's home was a long, two-storeyed building, a solid, granite farmhouse set in a square, with big iron gates at which a chained version of Leon set up a loud clamour at Hilario's approach. A man came running to open them, swearing at the dog, and he conducted Hilario, with Leon hugging close to his legs, into a huge kitchen, bright with oil lamps and the blaze of an open fire. There were also two round tables with braziers beneath them and therefore the room was pleasantly warm for all its size. Hilario, coming stingingly frozen from outside, began to feel uncomfortably hot.

There was no one in the room, which was occupied solely by a black cat that spat at Leon and fled into the yard before the door was shut, and Hilario's fears grew as he waited. He stroked Leon's head and tried to keep calm, but for some unknown reason his heart was beating very fast.

After an endless time seemed to have passed, Hilario jumped at the sound of footsteps. It was Don Agustín and he greeted the boy with proper courtesy, excusing his delay and offering him a warming drink. Then he turned to admire Leon and by this time there was much to admire, for the dog was larger than his own reputed sire, sturdier in build, and for all his dropped ears, with as much nobility and intelligence of expression as the pure-blooded wolf dog from Germany.

'What do you call him?' asked Don Agustín, and when Hilario told him he thoughtfully approved. 'Yes, he's as tough-looking as a lion and no doubt as valiant. But, to business.'

He then explained to Hilario that the examination results were in his hands, his because he happened to have associations with the hospital in question.

'I congratulate you,' he said. 'They're very good. Eighty-seven per cent. You're obviously intent upon your purpose, which is a trait I can admire in you because I share it.'

At any other time Hilario would have been overjoyed, but he knew that there was more to come and sensed that it would be less pleasant.

Don Agustín continued, 'But, as you will appreciate, a doctor requires more than intelligence. He must have a certain integrity, an ability to work hard, to understand people, to respect his superiors. In other words, the hospital require a character reference and they have asked me to supply it.'

Hilario said nothing, but he recalled a warning that someone – he could not remember whom – had called to him a long time ago, outside the church when he had quarrelled with this same man. 'He won't win the scholarship now, you'll see.' A sick feeling grew in his stomach and bitter anger stirred in his heart. He heard Don Agustín's words through a fog of mingled despair and rage, recognizing his own weakness and the other's strength.

It was so senseless. Don Agustín was already strong, just by his position, his wealth. No one had ever disputed it, any more than they would think to dispute their own position in the world, that of humble farmers and labourers, living by what they could drag hardily from the earth. But just because a boy of sixteen had found the courage to defy him, a boy of intellect and with great hopes of betterment, he felt his position threatened and sought to crush the spirit that had dared.

Don Agustín mentioned the great San Carlos hospital in Madrid. A nephew of his was one of its chief doctors; a recommendation from him could get Hilario a free scholarship there, with its greater advantages, whereas a negative recommendation from Don Agustín would shut the doors of even this Valladolid hospital to him for ever.

'Just think,' he said. 'The world is at your feet.'

'Is it so important for you to have my dog?' replied Hilario, his voice almost a whisper in its constraint.

'The unobtainable is always more attractive.'

He smiled. He was not even ashamed to show his weakness. Then he added briskly, 'Come now. It's not as if he wouldn't be well treated. And what would you do with him anyway, once you were away from home?'

'The holidays . . .' murmured Hilario vaguely. He hardly knew what he was saying.

It was not even for the dog. A much greater principle was at stake. Don Agustín himself had mentioned the word 'integrity', but it was obvious that to achieve his aim he must divest himself of all.

It was not the dog that mattered. . . . Hilario suddenly looked at Leon, anxiously watching him, sensing his master's turmoil. In this manner had those faithful dark eyes always watched him. He thought fleetingly of Nicolás, the shepherd with whom he had intended to leave the dog, knowing instinctively that with him Leon would make a new life and find a new happiness. It needed courage to defy those trusting eyes.

In the end, with a voice that he hardly recognized as his own, so strangled was he by various emotions, Hilario said, 'If I agree it's for the sake of my parents, not for me. They have sacrificed much for me and I can't destroy their faith in me now. It's not for the hospital. It's for what they have done for me.'

Don Agustín was very pleasant after that, admiring Hilario's good sense, his certain ability, but the lad was only anxious to escape and hardly heard his words. He understood the landowner's offer of a mule so that he could ride home in the cold darkness, but he shook his head and muttered something about preferring to walk.

He hardly looked at Don Agustín and could not even touch his dog. He made a rapid farewell to the former, bade Leon to 'stay' and almost ran from the room, drawing up against the icy outdoor air with a gasp of pain.

Tears stung in his eyes. He was glad of the darkness so that the man who opened the gate for him could not see them, and he trudged home almost enjoying the pain of coldness, trying not to feel at a loss without the dog at his side.

He imagined his parents' excited pleasure – his mother's doubt – when he told them the wonderful news about the hospital in Madrid. He knew that he could not have gone back home with Leon bearing bad news. They would never have understood and they would never have forgiven him. It was better to lose the dog's faith . . . there was no need to question it . . . but he was glad of the three-mile trek with the snow over his boots and his body turned to ice.

He resisted the urge to throw himself down into the snow and cry. He was a man now – soon to be a doctor – and men learned to keep their despair hidden within their hearts.

8: Vigil

It was impossible for Leon to understand his master's behaviour. He had understood well enough the command to stay
and obeyed it because Hilario had taught him very early in life
that disobedience was a dog's greatest sin. But before there had
been no need to question his commands. They had always
been reasonable. Now he sat where Hilario had left him,
watching the door through which he had rapidly vanished,
knowing that Don Agustín was watching him but ignoring

his gaze. Every moment he expected his master to return and his whole body quivered, ready for the command to follow which would surely come.

Don Agustín called to Leon several times, but the dog did not even flick his ears. His eyes were on the door and he hardly heard the man. Then he felt the man's hand softly on his head, scratching gently as had Hilario many a time. But it was not Hilario's hand and no other man had ever caressed him, not even the farmer who only took notice of the dog to curse him. The landowner spoke coaxingly, softly, but he had not Hilario's voice and the words meant nothing to the anxious dog.

Suddenly Don Agustín had an idea. A thick blanket hung beside the door which on cold days was usually pulled across to keep out the draughts. He walked across the room, switched the blanket across elaborately so that the dog should under-stand his meaning, then turned to look at Leon, his back to the door.

'Your master's gone,' he said. 'He won't come any more. You belong to me now.' He paused and then commanded, 'Leon, come here.'

Leon had watched him with interest. He was intelligent enough to realize that once the blanket was drawn the door would not open. He did not understand all the man's words but the tone of them was plain enough, especially the last command. This man was not his master, yet somehow he was.

Seconds passed as his animal brain tried to register the mean-ing of what had passed and finally, trained first in obedience, he stood up and went to the man who called him. But his gait was no longer carefree. He slunk to Don Agustín without looking at him, his tail almost between his legs.

The landowner praised and patted him for his obedience and then ordered Leon to follow him across the room to the other door. The dog did so, head miserably low. Bit by bit he was beginning to realize that Hilario had deliberately left him.

It was beyond him to understand why, but, in his complete faith in his master, he still expected him to return.

He followed Don Agustín to another room, a study heavy with books, swords and battle-axes and a suit of armour in one corner. It was occupied by two young men, sons of the land-owner, and the wolf dog, Leon's reputed sire.

Before the door was even shut and the man could speak there was a savage, snarling bark from the wolf dog and within a second the two animals were rolling over the floor, locked together, Leon crushed under the other, taken un-awares. A small table crashed over, books fell to the floor. Leon was on top now, but such was the flurry of move-ment that little damage was being inflicted. One of the sons was about to interfere when Don Agustín called him back sharply.

'Let them be. This should be interesting. Fritz always wel-comes newcomers in this way.'

The men drew back, moving several pieces of furniture and the glowing brazier out of the way at the same time. By now the dogs had broken away and were eyeing each other warily. Fritz had suddenly realized that here was an opponent even larger than himself; Leon was half stunned by the surprise of the first attack.

They growled, heads low, teeth bared, slowly circling each other. Leon was on the defence, not pugnacious by disposition and for the first time in his three years involved in battle. Fritz suddenly flung himself on the other dog again, viciously tearing at Leon's jaw, furiously jealous of the intruder that had entered meekly at his beloved master's heels.

Leon was away with a sharp twist of his head, diving to grab at a leg and throw the other off balance. Fritz was too quick for him and Leon yelped as his ear was torn open. Until now he had only been trying to defend himself, but the sharp pain drove him to equal rage and with a savage, throaty cry he threw himself with all his weight into an attack upon the other, fear, surprise and pain all forgotten as the desire to kill surged within him.

The small room was in a shambles, lost in a crescendo of snapping snarls and growls while the two animals tore at each other, urged on by the three men of whom they were completely unaware.

For the first time Fritz found himself fighting for his life. He felt Leon's slavering jaws near his jugular and dragged away. Teeth then dug into his lower jaw, pulling his head down in agony. He retaliated by crunching Leon's off foreleg. Both were scattering blood about the room and Don Agustín realized that it was time to stop them before they killed each other, both too proud to be vanquished.

At his word they were parted from each other by a rain of head blows from the men, each caught in strong arms before they could return to the battle. They growled and struggled and lunged at each other until Fritz was banished to the kitchen.

'Have a look at his wounds,' said Don Agustín to the son who took him and he himself bent to examine the panting Leon, who closed his eyes and turned away his head, wanting no attentions from him, however kind they might be.

Bright blood dripped from his ear, staining his shoulder, the floor and all that came in contact with it. His muzzle was chipped in various places and there was a deep bite over the left eye, although it hardly bled. The leg was badly bitten and caused Leon to limp for many days, but no permanent damage had been inflicted by either dog, except that they were undying deadly enemies and could never share a room. It was poor Fritz that was always banned, whimpering and alone in the kitchen, for Don Agustín was determined to gain the friendship of the village dog, so proud and reserved and unswerving in his loyalty to his former master.

2

Don Agustín had rarely come up against a man whom he could not defeat and he never expected to have to fight a battle of wills with a mere dog. That Leon should mope and be off his food for a day or so was normal, even more so after the savage battle he had given and the wounds that worried him. But the days went by and still the dog showed no sign of hunger, no sign of interest. He did nothing but lie and lick his injured leg, or sit and stare at the yard door if he were in the kitchen, turning his head away from any food that was placed before him.

He obeyed the landowner's commands, come, go, sit, stay and hackled up at the first sight of Fritz, but for the rest of the time he did nothing but mourn and with the passing of each day grew more listless. There was no way of stirring him from apathy, nor food that would tempt his appetite. He was offered meat in quantities that even Hilario would never have dreamed of, raw and sweet-smelling, but his nose did not even twitch.

Don Agustín watched him anxiously and often bad-temperedly. No one in the house could tempt him, not even his wife, who was fond of animals and whom Fritz adored and would have died for, not even his two small grandchildren, who played round the dog and tried to make him join their games.

Leon just sighed heavily from time to time, sounding so human in his patient sadness and ever watching the door through which Hilario must one day come to fetch him.

He was allowed out in the patio, but even the stingingly cold air and the bright sunshine could not move his sluggish blood. He would watch the road that led to the village, a whine dying in his throat on realizing that the gate barred it from him, and his intelligent eyes grew dull, his black nose grew dry and grey-looking, the sheen began to go from his thick, lion-coloured coat.

'He's just pining away,' Doña Cristina told her husband. 'Why not take him back to the boy?'

But Don Agustín was stubborn, as wooden-headed as the dog.

'He'll get over it,' he insisted. 'I've never known a dog to deliberately die of hunger yet.'

'But he's not even hungry!' exclaimed his wife impatiently. 'How long is it now? Five days?'

'He'll eat,' the man reiterated. 'He'll eat or . . .

'Or what? Do you think Fritz would be any different? would you expect him to be? Take him back. Leave him be. He can never be really yours.'

Don Agustín told her not to interfere. She had enough to look after with the house and the grandchildren. Women were sentimental and knew nothing about dogs like Leon.

One day he took Leon for long and strenuous exercise about his estate, loping behind his cantering horse, unable to escape because of the long lead that tethered him to a ring in the saddle. Not that Leon ever thought of escape, except wistfully. Hilario had left him here, had bade him to stay, and for all that it broke his heart he would obey. He returned exhausted from the run, swallowed long draughts of icy water almost choking, but the food put down for him he still refused to touch. He just threw himself down on the kitchen flagstones, near the yard door, and fell into a weary, feverish slumber, much broken by short whines and growls.

Doña Cristina came to see him and softly stroked his head, struck by the difference in his appearance after only a week. In her opinion the dog was actually dying and would do so if drastic action were not taken to save its life.

She attacked her husband furiously for his callous pride which would let a faithful dog die rather than admit that it had beaten him. Don Agustín sought excuses and reasons, enraged himself, and he began to curse the day he had ever coveted the village dog and regretted the means he had employed to possess him. Of these his wife knew nothing, although she did wonder aloud, 'I wonder what possessed the boy to sell him to you. Surely he must have loved the dog to inspire such devotion in return?'

'He needed the money,' retorted Don Agustín brusquely, And Doña Cristina cried, 'You men are heartless creatures.'

It was only due to the insistence of the generous-hearted Doña Cristina that Hilario was once again called to the land-owner's house. He returned with great reluctance, as much afraid this second time as he had been the first, ten days earlier.

This second time he was met in the yard by Doña Cristina. She was a small, tubby woman, very much like his own mother in many ways except that her clothes were much finer. Her speech was the same, practical, but there was per-haps more understanding in the gaze she directed at the tired-eyed young man, who, in his pale thinness and sullen ex-pression, looked more of a child to her than a soon to be enrolled medical student.

She said, 'Do you know why I've sent for you?'

'You, Doña Cristina? I thought it was Don Agustín with whom I had to speak.'

'No, my husband's not at home today. It's about the dog. We want you to take him home.'

Hilario said slowly, trying to hide all emotion, 'I gave my dog to Don Agustín. He's no longer mine to take.'

'He wants you to have him.'

She saw his hesitance and, suddenly angry, cried, 'It doesn't matter if you've already spent the money he paid you. The dog needs you. He'll die if you don't take him home.'

The terrible guilt, anxiety and loneliness that he had felt all these ten days showed plainly in Hilario's anguished face.

She said, more softly, 'Did you love him?'

Hilario nodded.

'Then why did you do it? Surely you could have found something else to sell.'

He said as respectfully as he could, trying to disguise his emotion, 'Don Agustín only wanted Leon.'

The dog was in the kitchen, cold for all that he was stretched out like a rug in front of the fireplace. He was as he had been for many days now, his muzzle on his paws, a bowl of food untouched nearby, his eyes watching the door – eyes that saw only mistily, the dog hardly even recalling the purpose of his vigil. When the door opened his ears no longer twitched. He was surrendering at last to the commencement of endless sleep and was almost completely unaware of his surroundings.

When he saw Hilario he could only look up at him with his eyes, too weak to move his head. The end of his tail waved faintly in greeting and, as his master kneeled beside him to gather the now almost light-weight body into his arms, the dry muzzle scratched against Hilario's cheek and the tongue crept out to touch him softly.

'Leon!'

The cry escaped Hilario in an uncontrollable sob of agony on seeing his so proud and beautiful companion dying upon the other man's hearthstone. He crushed the dog to him and bent his head over the almost brittle frame, ashamed that Doña Cristina should see the tears that soaked his cheeks.

9: Going away

Hardly a month had passed after Leon was brought back to the farmer's house when Hilario once again had to decide what he was going to do with his dog. This time the problem weighed very heavily with him, for now he knew the extent of Leon's love for him and could hardly hope for him to be happy in any place that he left him.

He had not expected Don Agustín to keep his word, but a

confirming letter had come from the hospital in Madrid, a letter that was proudly shown to everyone in the village by both parents in turn, and in January of 1936 he was to begin his first term as a student of medicine.

He had never explained to his parents why he had left Leon with the landowner, nor offered any reason for as suddenly bringing him home, almost as lifeless as when he had first found him. His mother accepted his devotion to the dog as she accepted everything about her son, without understanding but convinced that he was able enough to make his own decisions. The farmer, however, was more active in his censure of Leon's importance. He felt that there was something unmanly in being so sentimental about a mere animal and his disapproval showed in angry scowls whenever he saw the two together.

He would often remark, 'It's only a dog, after all,' and Hilario tried to make light of his father's derision, keeping Leon as much out of his way as possible.

But in the first few days of having him back in the house, when Leon had to be forcibly fed and was almost too weak to walk, the farmer could not help but see his son and the dog constantly together, the one tending upon the other, and he felt that the lad was wasting his time, wasting his family's time, which was more important in these last weeks of his being with them.

'You should go and see your Aunt Isabel, or your Uncle Frumencio. They'll surely give you a present,' and he named half a dozen more aunts and uncles to whom he was bound to wish farewell in good time.

Hilario was loath to go, anxious to avoid this obvious reminder that they must give him something, and he made his excuse Leon's illness, which gave his father more reason to vent his annoyance on the dog.

In the end he said, 'And when you go to Madrid that dog must go too. I've had enough of him in my house and I don't want him moping and whimpering because you're not here.'

Hilario replied, 'I'll take him to Nicolás. He'll be happy there.'

His father grunted scornfully. As if a dog's happiness mattered! There were enough human problems to be faced. By the time Hilario had studied doctoring for a couple of years he would realize that, too.

Hilario borrowed a mule to ride to his sister's home that last time and Leon came gambolling joyfully beside him. He was fit again, as strong and as beautiful as ever except for the ragged ear and the scarred eyebrow. He knew well the road to the shepherd's village and was glad to be going there.

The rutted fields were lost beneath the snow that had been falling intermittently for weeks and the only brightness was in a lone pine tree and the blueness of the almost cloudless sky. It was hard to believe that from such intense blueness should come such cold, but even the dog's thick blood could hardly resist it and only the pleasure of being with his master and on the road to Nicolás could make him forget his frozen pads and the frosty air that bit at his eyes and muzzle.

Hilario stirred the mule into a gallop where he could but it was a stubborn creature and rarely cared to exert itself beyond the clumsy, bone-breaking trot, regardless of the switch that slapped down on its neck and in spite of the cold.

There was beauty in the red sun burning icily from the heavens upon the white, empty plains, completely deserted; and pleasure in contemplating the joy of the dog that followed beside him, often looking up at him with faithful, loving eyes, pink tongue lolling, breath clouded with frost, and Hilario regained his happiness on that journey to the shepherd's house, knowing that the dog adored him too much ever to condemn any action of his.

He almost fell from the mule's back at the journey's end and stumbled on his brother-in-law's arm as he was led into the warm kitchen to be immediately surrounded by small nephews and friendly faces. He could tell Nicolás the truth of Don Agustín's apparent kindness and vent the bitterness and rage that had seethed silently within him for so long, and he could caress his dog openly and boast of Leon's fidelity.

Leon quickly made himself at home again, also, seeking out the shepherd's little bitch and appropriating for himself the few scraps that had been thrown down for her. She greeted him with her usual reserved pleasure, allowing him a lick or two of recognition, and she moved a little from her warm corner near the fireplace so that he could share it with her. Soon they were both asleep, the bitch with her head stretched across Leon's front legs, he with his head across her shoulders.

The next day he was following the shepherd to the sheep-pens, showing that he had forgotten nothing since the previous summer, a controlled excitement gleaming in his eyes and quivering in his muscles. Hilario was still in bed and for once Leon had not thought to wait for him. He took in the rank odour of the ewes with eager nostrils, circling carefully round them and working them into a thick bunch at one end of the pen, glancing back when he had done so for the shepherd's approval.

Nicolás allowed him to play with the flock for a while, although his own bitch showed disapproval by fidgeting at his side and once dashing to remonstrate with Leon, slashing at him with her teeth. She was well aware that the ewes could not escape from the pens, that Leon's eagerness to show his ability was in abuse of them, that he was keeping them from the food her master had brought them. She whined anxiously and looked with bewilderment at her master.

He understood and said to her softly 'Let him be.'

Hilario could spend no more than three days with the shepherd. He had come only to wish them good-bye and to

leave Leon. He hoped that this time Leon would understand.
It was impossible to explain that he must go away until the
summer. Such words had no meaning to a dog.

He himself put a rope round Leon's neck and tied him in the
yard, much as he had done previously when first he had gone
to Valladolid. He hoped that like this the dog would understand that from now on this must be his home.

Leon watched him ride away, kicking the mule into a
furious gallop that lasted about a minute but which was
enough to get him away from the village. The dog watched
him with anxious eyes, Nicolás standing beside him with a
hand gently caressing his skull and ears. He watched silently
until Hilario and the mule were about the size of a bird on the
silent, frosty plain, and then he jumped forward with a whine,
stopped by the rope jerking at him. He dropped to all fours
and bayed deeply, but the smeared figures on the white landscape grew only more distant and then vanished.

Nicolás untied the rope and brought Leon into the house.
He kept him in the kitchen until the early afternoon, when it
was time to take more fodder to the sheep. Both dogs went
with him, eager at his heels, and Leon showed his usual interest
and excitement in the presence of the ewes. Nicolás was aware
of him moving about in the gathering darkness, first one side
and then another, sometimes alone and sometimes with the
bitch, but when he called them both back to the house, Leon
had disappeared.

Hilario's mother was packing the suitcase when Leon
arrived back in the village, making his presence known by
loud, excited barks. Hilario was both pleased and very cross.
He checked his first desire to greet Leon with joy and scolded
him sternly for not staying with the shepherd. Leon hung his
head, lifting his eyes mournfully to his master, but Hilario
refused to be overcome by the piteous gaze at which his dog
was so adept.

He was to go away the very next day and had no time to return the dog to Nicolás. His father was in the house, bound to be stirred to annoyance by this new action of the dog. He went back into the kitchen, shutting Leon out in the patio, to tell them what had happened.

'Leave him out there,' said the farmer. 'He'll soon grow tired of hanging around in this cold. Let him find his own way back to Nicolás and leave us in peace.'

Hilario resented his father's harshness towards the dog but could not defy him. He heard Leon whining in the patio and scraping at the door. Several times his father went out and drove him away with the threat of blows, but Hilario did not stir from the house, afraid to see the dog again.

That evening most of his various relations came to wish him good-bye and there was talk and laughter and some tears until late into the night. Hilario took part in the conversation and pretended gaiety, but beyond the buzz of talk his ears were straining for some sound of Leon.

Twice he went out into the yard. The first time he saw Leon lying at a short distance, hardly more than a heavy shadow in the weak light that filtered through the kitchen window from the oil lamp. Master and dog stared at each other, then Hilario turned his back and returned to the kitchen. The second time he looked almost furtively for the same faithful shadow, but it had gone.

2

Leon went back to the shepherd. Now he knew that Hilario had rejected him and that no more in that house, to which he had been brought and where first he had known kindness, would he find shelter or welcome. He could not reason his master's behaviour towards him and so could only accept it. Being a dog used to certain comforts the thought of hanging about the village rubbish dump to gain his sustenance did not even occur to him. He knew that in the shepherd's house he

would find that which was denied him here, but he returned
to the other village with less spirit than when he had set out
and, on arrival, gave no joyful barks of greeting nor sought
their welcome.

He arrived some time after midday and hung about the
yard until the door opened and Nicolás came out, cloaked in a
thick cape and with the bitch at his heels as always, off to feed
the sheep. The shepherd exclaimed at the sight of him and
would have greeted him warmly, but Leon avoided his touch,
satisfied just to fall in behind him in the company of the little
mongrel, wanting neither words nor sympathy. He was
dispirited, weary too with some thirty miles of travelling in so
short a time, and demonstrated no interest in the ewes. He
followed the mongrel back to the house and flopped himself
down in her usual place.

The children crowed with delight at the sight of him and
the youngest came toddling with fierce determination to pull
his whiskers and twist his ears, all of which Leon had learned
to tolerate. The child was pulled away by his mother, but,
although she called Leon and would have greeted him fondly,
his eyes stared into the fireplace and he did not even prick his
ears.

He dozed for several hours and woke with a start at the
chink of plates and glasses. The little mongrel was wandering
about the chairs and under the table, snapping up bits that the
children dropped and waiting for the occasional scrap to be
slyly or deliberately slipped to her.

Nicolás had the youngest child on his knee as he ate. He saw
that Leon was watching him and called to him, snapping his
fingers for him to come. But Leon looked away and stayed
where he was, stirring only when a battered saucepan was
pushed under his nose at the end of the meal containing a few
stewed lentils and a pig's knuckle-bone.

He swallowed the lentils and gnawed sporadically at the
bone, watched enviously by the bitch, but took no notice of

the children being prepared for bed, an activity which usually caught his attention and amused him.

When Nicolás went to take his last look at the sheep for the night, both dogs followed him. He called to Leon, but the dog had no wish for attention and ignored him. Once Nicolás saw him staring in the direction that Hilario had taken to return to the village, but it was only for a second and then Leon was trotting off somewhere with the little bitch, for the first time in his life completely independent.

10: War

Leon grew fond of Nicolás. He did not love the shepherd in the way that he had loved Hilario – to no one could he ever give that kind of devotion again – but the everyday association between the man and the dog, the many hours in each other's company, sharing the same work and lunch, brought them to an understanding which became affection. The shepherd still loved his little mongrel more than Leon. He admired the wolf dog for his many qualities, he spoke to him and caressed him equally, but the bitch had been his companion for too many years to replace her so lightly in his heart.

Out on the plain, rough here with hillocks and huge boulders and wiry grass already well nibbled, Nicolás would sit with a dog on either side of him and the three would half doze in the hot sunshine of late spring, the occasional blurred jangle of sheep bells sounding soothingly in their ears. But Leon and his master always had at least one eye on the ewes, even though the bitch would curl up into sound slumber from time to time.

No word was needed from Nicolás to guide Leon in his care of the flock. From a seemingly heavy doze he would be up in a flash to bring back a straying lamb or haze up the limping ones that always got left behind.

But for Nicolás there was no hand-licking or adoring gazes from those dark, intelligent eyes. Leon watched the sheep and occasionally teased the little bitch. And there was no gay dancing about the shepherd as they followed him each morning at the start of the daily round, nor barks of joy. The joy had gone out of Leon with Hilario's rejection of him and none other than he could bring it back.

His fondness for Nicolás remained a secret thing within him. It made him stop with the shepherd and be faithful to him, caring for his sheep; it made him tolerant with the young children who kicked and pummelled him and pulled his ears; but it was not great enough to make him demonstrate it in any way beyond this, following him, obeying him, preferring him to another.

When the summer came Leon noticed that the people in the house were no longer as happy as they had always been. Where there had been laughter and chattering in the evenings, with the children dashing restlessly about watched by the dogs from their corner, a tenseness had come to replace the laughter which was no longer heard. Once the shepherd's wife was crying and Nicolás had been unable to comfort her. Both dogs had flattened their ears at the sound of her sadness, and the little bitch had whined dolefully. She too sensed that happiness had gone out of the house and she clung closer than ever to her master, feeling that his fondness for her was ebbing too.

On the plain Nicolás would fondle both dogs absently, sighing heavily, and now he no longer noticed Leon's cleverness with the sheep nor praised him for work well done. One day the shepherd suddenly took hold of the little bitch by her front legs and held her up close to him, much as he did with his own children at times. He then pressed her against him, bowing his head over her for a long time, before remarking with bitter sadness, 'And you, too, what will you do without me?'

Then he saw Leon watching him, the dark eyes expressing puzzlement. Leon was a magnificent animal now, tall, thick, heavy with tawny hair, bright with intelligence. Nicolás stared at him for several seconds, admiring the strength and sagaciousness of him, and then he said, 'You'll have to look after them, Leon. I shall leave them all with you.'

The dog pricked his ears, head slightly cocked. He knew that the man wanted something of him, but he could not understand what it was. Everything was bewildering to Leon these days. Although the summer was as all summers, the sun achingly hot and the ground exhaustingly dry and they dozed in the afternoons in the generous shadow of a clump of pines or boulders, slothful as always in July and August, there was tension in the heat and even fear.

One day a boy came to share the long hot days with Nicolás and the dogs, and the shepherd spent much of the time explaining things to him, pointing out the different terrains, good and bad, telling him about the sheep and the dogs.

Leon listened while the little bitch slept. For all that she sensed her master's troubles, nothing could keep her from sleeping. Her muzzle was grizzling with age and she was too sure of him ever to think of losing him. But Leon, without understanding the words, somehow sensed that Nicolás was handing over the care of his flock to this boy, a cousin of his no more than ten or twelve years old.

For many days the shepherd taught the boy and Leon listened with pricked ears and curious eyes, unused to so much talk, while the little bitch grunted and twitched at the fleas that bit her as she slept.

There came a night when no one went to bed until it was almost morning. It was a terrible night, filled with a sadness that crushed the two dogs, subdued the noisy children and left the shepherd and his wife almost speechless. When at last the children were undressed for bed, and they queued up as usual for the last-minute kiss and blessing from their father, he held them close to him as Leon had seen him hold the dog and there were tears on his cheeks as he wished them good night.

The next morning Nicolás did not take out the sheep. There was a shabby canvas bag on the kitchen table with a few of his things in it and, very early, a rickety lorry stopped outside the door, already filled with men who called out for the shepherd, pretending to be jovial. Nicolás gave his last hurried good-byes to his family and, stopping in the doorway as he was about to leave, he glanced at Leon and said, 'Look after them for me. One day I'll come back.'

Then he was gone, pulled up into the lorry by those already there, and the woman was in the doorway crying and waving, surrounded by the children who also waved and looked serious.

There was a sharp bark from the little mongrel as she suddenly realized that her master was going away without her. She dashed through the door and followed after the lorry, scurrying as fast as her short legs would carry her. The woman called to her in vain and neither could Nicolás, shouting at her from the lorry, make her desist. She followed as she had always followed, the dust from the lorry blinding her and choking her throat.

Through the village she went, barking wildly, and out on to the plain. Leon stood at the door with the woman and the

children and watched her until she disappeared from sight.
She never returned and neither did her master.

2

The war which was to batter Spain for three exhausting years,
and which took the shepherd and his dog as well as many
others, made its effects felt in even the smallest of villages, in-
habited mainly by women, old people and children. Even the
animals knew the difference when all their masters were gone
and there were only women or boys to jerk the mule reins and
jab the oxen into movement.

Leon did not go out on the plain with the sheep any more.
The shepherd had told his wife to keep him about the house,
saying that he would worry less about them if he could know
that Leon was there to guard them. The little bitch knew
enough about the sheep to help the young lad with them, but
the bitch had run off with her master and the boy must care
for them alone, for the woman was determined not to lose
Leon also.

She put a rope round his neck and tied him to a staple in the
wall beside the kitchen door, where the size of him would
warn off unwelcome visitors. Busy with her four young
children and thinking only of her husband who had gone
away, she had no time to worry about Leon beyond feeding
him, and a different life began for the mongrel wolf dog
tethered night and day beside the door.

He fretted loudly at first, whining and barking and tugging
at the rope, unused to such constant and endless confinement,
but the woman was accustomed to the screams of her children
and took no notice of the dog. He would quieten down after
a day or so.

So he did. He quietened into listless moping, livening only
when someone came out to the yard, ever hopeful that release
would be coming with them. But it would only be the
woman with slops to throw out and she hardly spared the dog

a glance, or the boys coming to play when it was better that he should not be noticed, for they were persistent tormentors at times.

The summer passed drearily for Leon. He dreamed of his lost masters and he dreamed of the sheep, whining in his sleep, and his legs grew stiff because he made no use of them. The rope was hardly more than the length of his body and, to pass the time, Leon took to digging holes through the straw into the hard earth of the patio. The hens would come and peck at what he had dug up and Leon would lie very still, watching them as once he had watched the sheep. So still would he be that they would almost come between his front paws to scratch, and their busy movement would bring a brightness to his eyes for a while.

Winter came and then it was that the ewes really lacked a shepherd, for the carrion crows were hungry and the boy knew nothing of lambing. More than half the new crop of lambs was lost and several of the ewes also. The scent of the sheep penned near the house excited Leon and for a while he forgot that he was a prisoner, breathing in the smell of them and listening to their bleatings.

The cousin came to live in the house and he brought with him a dog of his own, a gangling, half-starved creature of some hunting breed, good for starting up hares and holding to their course but hopeless with the ewes. Even the boy realized this and after a while left her in the house when he went out to the sheep.

It was so cold at night-time that the shepherd's wife at last took pity on Leon, shivering in the yard, and let him sleep in the kitchen again as had been his custom. The two animals crept close to the cinders dying in the fireplace and passed the coldest hours in reasonable comfort, but as soon as the woman had risen in the morning she tied Leon out in the yard again, afraid of losing him as she had lost the other dog.

By early spring the hunting dog had a litter of five puppies and soon they were all over the house, dragged about by the children. They got under everyone's feet, dirtied all the floors and chewed up things that should not be touched, and the woman was weary with children and puppies and worrying about her husband. She would have got rid of the hunting dog but that the boy was fond of her and refused to look after the sheep if he could not keep her, and eventually she threw them all out to the yard and tied up the mother dog at a good distance from Leon.

She discovered that the bitch was far better at warning of the approach of anyone than was Leon. The wolf dog only moped the whole day long and hardly cared who came or went from the house, whereas the other set up a clamour at everyone who passed by the door. Even she with her un-observant eyes could see that Leon was degenerating in both looks and disposition. Careless feeding was affecting his skin and when he was not dozing he was scratching furiously, leaving raw patches that attracted the flies. Boredom affected the brightness of his eyes and he lost that eager, questioning expression that had always enhanced his general appearance, while the constant teasings of the four children and their friends were beginning to affect his temper.

She was astonished the first time she heard him growl at the approach of the baby of the family, for Leon had always been the most tolerant of dogs and fond of the children. After that she kept a closer eye on him and if she heard him growl, or saw him show his teeth in warning, she would rush out to hit him and pull the child away. She told the children to leave him alone, but was too easy-going with them to insist that they obey her instructions and, once they realized that Leon repre-sented a certain danger, he became a challenge to the bravery of most of the young boys of the village.

He was so big, he growled so fiercely at times, his teeth were so large and shiny, that he was awesome enough for most of the five- and six-year-olds, but he was also limited in his reach and the test of bravery was to see who would linger longest and nearest while rousing him to anger.

There were times when he had a crowd of seven or eight boys dancing about him, teasing him in every imaginable way. For a long time he would endure in silence, but suddenly he would spring to all fours, barking furiously, and the boys would scatter like chaff in the wind, utterly terrified. But back they would creep, pretending some days that he was a bull, and they would bring a tattered rag to flap at him and jab at him with sticks doing service as swords.

The other dog was already so crushed, whimpering but accepting anything that was done to her, that she was no challenge and was soon left alone. Her puppies were carried off or killed in the yard, yelping in vain, for there was no one who cared enough to help them.

One day Leon bit the smallest child. It was only a very small bite, hardly a graze on his fingers, and the dog had not meant to draw blood nor even realized that he had done so. He had snapped sharply as the little boy came rushing at him with a broom and somehow the two had collided.

The boy screamed in fright rather than pain, but the mother was terrified, thinking of rabies, although it was too early in the year for the heat that brought out such an illness in the village dogs. She rushed the still screaming child from neighbour to neighbour, seeking the best advice, and when at last she had been calmed and some iodine was dabbed on the graze, she could think only of Leon's treachery.

'After being cared for so long and fed twice a day! Who would think that my brother's dog could do such a thing! We've obviously been too kind to him and this is the way he repays us!'

Leon was dozing in what was left of the afternoon's weak sunshine when the shepherd's wife came back to the house full of righteous indignation, the little boy in her arms and the other children crowding around her. His peaceful state was in such contrast to the agony of fear she had lived through only an hour earlier and drove her to new rage against him.

'It's no good treating an animal with kindness,' she cried. 'They don't understand it,' and, watched with big eyes by the children, she found an old belt of her husband's, doubled it and beat the dog until he yelped and cringed and lay still under the blows, no longer trying to escape them.

The little boy began to cry. In his brutal way he was fond of Leon and it was he who brought the dog's punishment to an end by rushing up and throwing his arms round Leon's neck, crying, 'No, Mama, no. Don't hit him any more.'

Leon was left alone then and the children were promised a similar whipping if they touched him again. The yard was suddenly almost deserted as they rushed off to play somewhere else and the woman went into the house.

The sun had gone and the chill of evening was creeping through the village and up to the walls of the houses. Leon, with his back to the wall, stretched his muzzle across his hind legs in preparation for sleep, but he did not shut his eyes.

He had only ever once been deliberately beaten in his life and that had been three years earlier when he had chased the sheep and deeply angered his master. He had borne no grudge against Hilario, knowing that the boy loved him and that he had offended him seriously. But this time he had no knowledge of his crime, unaware even that he had brought blood to the young child's hand, and the whipping had left him utterly bewildered.

With the gathering dusk resentment grew. Deserted by the only one he had ever loved, abandoned by Nicolás, mercilessly teased by the children and beaten without cause by the shepherd's wife, Leon's natural affection towards them all began to fade. While his body ached, rebellion filled him.

11: A new master

It was a sad spring for the shepherd's wife. First came the news of her husband's death in battle and shortly afterwards she learned that her brother had been the victim of an air-raid on Madrid. There was no one to come back to Leon and, having the other dog big and noisy enough to act as guardian, she accepted the first offer to buy him. The man to whom she sold him gave her next to nothing, but she was glad not to have to

see the dog any more, reminding her of the two people who
had brought the most joy to her house.

Leon could hardly believe it when she came to untie the
rope, nor was he happy when the loose end was put into a
strange man's hands and the gruff order, 'Come', was issued
to him. He resisted for a moment, not out of affection for the
woman who had sold him but in natural distrust of his new
owner and a disinclination to leave the only home he now
knew.

As the man pulled on the rope, the woman shooed at him
and one of the children smacked him across the rump. Leon,
spiritless now and, after the first instant, hardly caring,
obeyed the newly commanding voice and the rope went
slack as he meekly surrendered. He followed the stranger out
of the yard, head drooping, not even excited about being
released from eternal tethering.

There was a small, donkey-drawn cart beside the house. Its
axle was at about the level of Leon's head. The man tied the
loose end of the rope to an iron ring that hung beside the axle
in the centre of the cart and then he left Leon to go about his
business in the village.

The waiting dog sniffed at the iron-rimmed wheels, stared
up at the boards above his head from which dangled wisps of
straw and from which permeated a rank odour of smoked
herrings, vinegar and rats. The shepherd's children hung about
the cart for a while, watching Leon and the donkey, but they
went away when their mother called and the dog fell into a
doze.

The man came back. When Leon did not stir at the sound
of his footsteps he poked the dog to all fours. Then he jumped
up on to the cart, whacked the donkey's rump with a broom-
stick and set off at a fast trot along the cart-track that led to the
next village some six miles distant which was where he lived.

Leon was startled. Unaccustomed to this manner of travel,
at first he could not even understand who or what was drag-

ging him along. The rope was tied short, so that he had to keep up with the donkey's pace, and in his bewilderment he was unable to catch the rhythm, finding it impossible to keep up with the swaying cart without half strangling himself for being too far behind or almost getting his toes run over by the wheels.

The man suddenly realized the dog's predicament. Had he been a good-hearted fellow he would have slowed the donkey to a walk until Leon could learn the trick of pacing in the centre between the two wheels, but Leon's new owner was mean-natured and even cruel. He found the dog's unhappy bewilderment very amusing and, with a laugh, beat the donkey into a gallop, crying out to Leon, 'You'll learn. You'll learn.'

The donkey fled from its master's beatings; the cart bounced over the ruts in the track, almost unseating its driver at times, and Leon struggled and surrendered in turn, hardly knowing how to escape this tortuous journey nor what had split asunder the endless tranquillity of his eventless life. It was not difficult to keep the donkey's pace, as his legs were long, but the dust choked him, and the cart lurched, dragging him from side to side, buffeting his hind end against the spinning wheels, smacking his head on the axle.

The nightmare experience terrified him and soon he was howling in fear and pain, loping along but constantly being grazed by the wheel or the axle. He was blinded by dust that spurted into his eyes, nose and ears and was thoroughly exhausted.

Eventually the man yanked the donkey to a halt and again Leon crashed his head into the axle. He sank to the ground, panting and dripping sweat from his foam-streaked, dust-caked jaws, his tawny head stained with blood and his hind-quarters aching with bruises. His eyes were shut, but they opened quickly as he felt the presence of the man beside him.

With an oath, the man grabbed the rope round his neck and

dragged Leon from under the cart. He could see that the dog was all in, for, even though he kicked him, Leon did not rise. He shrank from the blow but continued to pant heavily.

The man was short, hardly more than five feet tall, but he was broad and stocky and very strong. He untied the rope from the ring, gathered Leon in his arms and flung him into the cart. He then re-tethered him to the cart itself and once again whipped up the donkey.

On reaching his destination he shut up both the dog and the donkey in a small dark outhouse which served as a stable and Leon had until the following morning to recover from his battering. He was left alone till then, the man not even coming to feed him. The donkey champed on a forkful of musty straw, thick with thistle burrs, and the dog went hungry.

2

Leon had never been deliberately ill-treated before. He had been beaten in punishment only rarely; he had felt hunger when there had been little for him to eat; he had even been neglected by the shepherd's wife and teased by her children; but there had always been a certain amount of affection for him and a feeling of belonging on his part. Never before had he felt so utterly friendless and alone and even afraid.

His master, Rubio, was a middle-aged man who made a living selling olives, smoked herrings and sardines and a few other odds and ends in the villages. He would go to the nearest town with his donkey, buy a big barrel of green olives and another of black, and half a dozen round boxes of smoked fish. He would sell them in small quantities, four herrings at this house, two at the next, a dozen sardines a little farther on, and some women would want a lot of olives and some only a few. By the time he had emptied both barrels and boxes he had recovered his initial expenses three times over, and when he was not selling olives and fish he had a piece of land to till and vines to care for.

He lived alone in a small cottage on the outskirts of the village and apart from being small and mean-natured, he was also ugly and had no friends. He was always afraid that some-one might steal his donkey or his merchandise and therefore he kept a dog tied to the cart when he was about his business, to guard it for him. He never made friends with his dogs, even though he was so much alone.

If anyone told him not to beat his donkey so much, nor to treat his dogs so roughly, he would laugh, but his anger would stay inwards until the person had gone away and then he would thrash the donkey more or kick the dog about to relieve his rage. As it was never difficult to find a dog, he hardly bothered to care for them. If one died, within a week or so he could obtain another, and if he paid the shepherd's wife for Leon it was only because the wolf dog was the biggest he had ever seen and he had only ever owned small dogs be-fore.

At first Leon accepted his new life without rebellion. He had enough to occupy him in learning to keep pace with the cart without hurting himself. He was quickly tired, for he was always ravenously hungry and the food he was given was hardly enough to keep a cat alive. When he was not tied to the cart he was locked in the shed so that he had no opportunity to scrounge food for himself. Even the occasional mouse he was wary of chasing, for his companion, the donkey, was such a nervous creature that the slightest unexpected movement would have it lashing out with hard hind hooves. After almost having his ribs broken on one occasion, Leon learned to be very wary and preferred to let the mice escape than be kicked again.

But he endured. Within a week he was as accustomed to his place under the cart as if it had been his from birth. The only time he banged his head on the axle was when the donkey stopped abruptly or unexpectedly and this was only because he was tall and the cart was small. Had he been a smaller dog his head would never have reached the axle, but the fact that he had a constantly bruised and split skull caused no anxiety to his new master.

He even grew accustomed to the dark rankness of the filthy outhouse and to sleeping on soggy straw that crawled with insects and worms of every kind. At first Rubio had had to drag him into the shed, Leon resisting all the way in spite of blows and kicks, and he had even welcomed the approach of the man in the morning if only to release him from the foulness of his prison. The dog who had once slept on his master's bed was made as much miserable by such squalor as by any number of kicks and blows which fell upon him unreasonably, just because he happened to be within his master's reach.

The only enlightenment in his miserable life was the daily journeying from village to village, when for several hours at least the man concentrated on beating his donkey and selling his wares and Leon was more or less forgotten under the cart. He could relax undisturbed while women flocked about and the fresh air, smelling of spring flowers, was a balm after the rankness of the stable. But his pads were bruised by sharp stones and he was constantly attacked by a ravening thirst which was only satisfied at night at the donkey's trough, so that no respite could be entirely pleasant.

Several weeks went by and there was no one who would have recognized Leon as the dog that Don Agustín had coveted, nor the companion so dearly loved of Hilario. He was gaunt and dirty. His coat was dull and patchy, but the biggest changes of all were in his expression and carriage. Once joy and intelligence had gleamed from his dark eyes, expressing itself in his gaily held tail, his prancing steps, the alert position of his head. Now he slunk, cringing at the man's approach in expectation of the blow that usually accompanied it, and his eyes were narrow and dull.

His innate respect for man's omnipotence had tarnished rapidly. There was neither love, nor affection, nor even a way of accepting that he belonged to this man, nor the man to him. The man was a brute, as he was, but an even lesser creature than Leon because the dog was intelligent and had been generous by nature.

It took Leon three or four weeks to realize that the man was not even his equal and when he understood this all Hilario's training rapidly vanished from his memory. Fear ruled here, not obedience, and one morning when Rubio came to release the dog and the donkey from the shed, cursing as usual and free with his blows, Leon flew at him with a strangled growl, bowling him to the ground as he sought for a hold on his throat.

The dog and the man rolled over and over together, fighting frenziedly. Leon was mad with hatred and hunger and he attacked Rubio as if it were Fritz he was fighting, his instinctive respect for the human race utterly crushed by this man's treatment of him.

Rubio beat at him with his short, heavy arms, certain that the dog must be rabid. One hand desperately sought for a weapon while the other kept the dog from his throat, and at last his fingers clung to a heavy stone. With all his strength he crashed it down on Leon's skull. The dog grunted and fell slack, rolling off the man's body with jaws still open.

The man scrambled to his feet, but Leon did not move, even though Rubio gave him a heavy kick to make sure that he was as dead as he looked. Rubio was trembling. His clothes were torn and there were scratches on his face and chest. There were bites on his left wrist and hand which bled profusely.

He returned to the house, cleaned his injuries with raw alcohol and sought about for a reasonably clean rag with which to bandage his hand. The dog's mouth had looked clean enough so that his fear of rabies had subsided, to be replaced by his brutal rage.

He smacked the dirt out of his clothes, then went to fetch the donkey which he harnessed to the cart with the maximum of punches and curses. He then gave the inert dog yet another kick before picking him up and throwing him into the cart. The donkey, anticipating the first beating of the morning, was already on his way when Rubio jumped up and took the reins.

12: Killer dog

When Leon opened his eyes he was aware of three things: heat, silence and pain. He shut his eyes again quickly as sunlight stabbed through them, then slowly opened them a second time. The midday sun seemed to have sucked the last ounce of moisture from his beaten, skeletal frame and the stiff muscles could hardly obey his will to move.

Pain shot through him as he made an effort to pull himself to all fours and he collapsed in the surprise of it. He made another effort and, with some difficulty, stood upright, swaying, dizzy, head low and the breath rasping through his half-open jaws. When he had accustomed himself to the pain that the broken rib caused him, and some of the dizziness had faded, he was able to take note of his whereabouts.

He was at the bottom of a steep basin, huge, bleached bones scattered on either side of him, and apart from a few blow-flies that buzzed round his head – noisy now that the dog's movements had disturbed them – he was the only living creature there. Believing him to be dead, Rubio had tossed him into the animal graveyard, a place some three miles from the village to which were taken all the old donkeys, mules, oxen, or sick animals that died mysteriously and whose flesh could not be eaten. Crows and carnivorous insects came to strip the meat from the bones and the sun quickly turned them brittle and white. But the hungry dogs and cats kept away. It was a place that frightened them.

Leon, too, sensed the all-pervading atmosphere of death. It caused his hackles to rise automatically and he snarled softly in his throat while looking warily from side to side. He recognized his own weakness, which was great. He could hardly move in his stiffness, his body battered both by Rubio's boots and the fall from the cart from the top of the ridge to this hollow some fifteen feet below. He still swayed slightly, standing fearfully there.

He saw that to escape he would have to cross the whole length of the graveyard. On the other side was a low, easily assailable slope, and it was with dragging, wincing movements that he traversed the graveyard, giving the remains there as wide a berth as possible. The flies buzzed angrily about his head and he hardly cared.

They left him as he limped up the slope into the comparatively fresh, though heat-laden air of the open plain. At the top of the ridge Leon stopped, his jaws wide, breath grabbed painfully by his bruised lungs and pressing on the broken rib. In front of him stretched the whole plain of Castilla, deserted, silent; green, brown and ochre yellow. It went on to the horizon with hardly a tree or a wall or a cart track and not a single house. It was as vast and as empty as the blue hot sky above him and Leon, sick and weary, was afraid of its emptiness.

The earth that had been warm and gentle, inviting and

exciting in his walks with Hilario long ago, now was hard and hostile, rejecting him as the humans had rejected him, one by one. Where was he to go, in which direction was there any promise? Every side offered the same vista and at his back was the graveyard. It was the only tangible thing, however horrific, in all the emptiness that surrounded him and for this reason alone Leon was loath to step forward and leave it behind.

Regathering the little strength that remained to him, the dog circled the graveyard, coming eventually to the top of the ridge from which he had been thrown by Rubio. From this point the land undulated down to the village in which Leon had known such wretchedness. The small houses were toy-like in aspect from such a distance and there were very few of them. In one of them lived Rubio, the man who had made such a terrible impression upon Leon.

Beyond the village the emptiness again took up its sway and there was nothing but unchecked plains, spring green and cloud shadowed, parted by a dusty ribbon of cart-track. The track would end in a village as they all did. In one such village was the shepherd's wife. For a moment the memory tempted Leon. He whined softly, forgetting the children who teased and hurt him, remembering only Nicolás and the little bitch and the times when the woman had been kinder to him. He started forward suddenly, dull eyes bright for a second, and the pain that stabbed a yelp out of him reminded him that Nicolás was no longer there and that the woman had betrayed him to Rubio. He halted and his eyes dulled again. In this direction also there was nothing.

A breeze danced about on the hill-top, ruffling the bedraggled feathers of the dog's tail. Leon's dry nose twitched as automatically he inhaled its carried scents and then he whined again in excitement, for the breeze stirred other memories, told him of other places.

Further south, far beyond his vision, was yet another village;

the one in which he had been born and reared, the one in which had lived his god. The breeze had come a long way, tumbling through young corn and bright poppies, blowing across the barren stretches. Leon drank it in eagerly, whimpering in excitement, suddenly no longer alone and afraid. He pricked his ears, lifted his tail. . . . Just as suddenly he drooped again. There was no Hilario.

Head bowed, Leon stood on the ridge and let the breeze tug about him. He no longer noticed it and his dry nose was motionless. On this side, too, the plain offered him all that it could ever offer to the homeless and unwanted: a long journey through loneliness, a long journey to nowhere. This realization defeated Leon. He had experienced many aspects of man's character and suffered as well as enjoyed, but from the very first moments his life had always been guided and ruled by man. For good or bad he had belonged to human society and his life had been lived as ordained by that society.

Alone on the ridge, masterless, rejected, he had no one to command him or arrange his days. He was utterly free to do as he wished, but his freedom was an illusion, for his spirit was chained to man. All the earth was his and the vastness of it frightened him, for there was nowhere for him to go. His distress escaped in sobs that choked his throat. He wanted Hilario to call him; Nicolás; even the boys who teased him, but there was only the open plain and its very silence seemed to call him, dragging him unwillingly to its freedom.

When at last Leon left the hill-top it was in a southerly direction. The wheatlands to the south were no different in aspect from those to the north, but at least in the former hung the memory of Hilario's voice.

2

Leon soon discovered that an ownerless dog was completely unprotected. He had returned to Rubio's village, while keeping well away from the man's house, scavenging on the out-

skirts for whatever food he could find. For several days the
pain of the broken rib and his general bruised condition had
left him without appetite, but, as soon as he began to recover
a little, hunger returned with ravenous insistence. Where there
were people there was food, and the dog sought desperately
among the dust and ashes of the rubbish heaps, gulping down
whatever even smelled slightly edible. An hour later, his
hunger somewhat appeased in his uneasy stomach, he brought
up everything he had swallowed and was worse off than
before.

He returned to the rubbish heap and, so intent was his
search, he had no thought for caution. A woman who had
come to empty her rubbish on the heap threw a broken brick
at him, thinking of the chickens that ran about the alleys and
struck by Leon's famished appearance. It was enough to drive
him away with a yelp of pain, but later he was back again in
unfruitful search.

The history of the next few weeks was unchanging. The
constant hunger which rubbish dumps could hardly ease, the
constant expectation of cuts and bruises from the humans who
would drive him away, afraid of unknown strays, that might
steal their hens or, worse, be carriers of the dreaded rabies. The
rubbish dump was for their own hungry dogs, not for strays
as fearful in aspect as Leon, tall, big-jawed and gaunt, wild
about the eyes.

Loneliness and hunger brought him eventually back to the
shepherd's village and the house where once he had known
contentment of a kind. The woman hardly recognized him at
first and even when she did and cried his name there was only
fear and horror in her voice. She dashed back to the house and
came out with a broom. Leon backed away from her, understanding but hardly believing. It took a crack across the skull
to convince him and he fled yelping down the street, his tail
between his legs. Some boys saw his flight and chased after
him, shouting with glee. They threw handfuls of stones after

him, which hardly hurt but encouraged him not to relax his speed.

He learned to come to the rubbish dumps in the very early morning or during the hottest hours of the afternoon when no one was about, and experience taught him to be wary of jagged tins and broken glass. But this manner of existence was for Leon a miserable affair. He had lived too well for too long to be able to accept this cringing lingering on the fringe of human society, a target for anyone who chose to go for him, unwanted everywhere.

After a few weeks, stronger for all that hunger ruled his life, he was able to face the aspect of the open plain with less dread. His attempts to find a place for himself on the outskirts of the villages had reminded him of what he had already learned and forgotten several times.

But ingrained habit was a difficult thing to break. He had compromised with freedom, choosing to live on the outskirts of humanity, a part of it without belonging, and he learned the hard way that he never would belong and yet he never would be free. In a short while he grew accustomed to liberty and, instead of looking upon an owner as a desired but unobtainable luxury, he began to see humans as an enemy, creatures to outwit and avoid and never to trust.

When at last he could look upon the human race as something he no longer needed his independence was complete. The vast stretches of wheatlands again seemed friendly and inviting. He had memories of chasing hares across the stubble and, for one who had the dust and dirt of villages sticking to his nostrils, the winds blew fresh and inviting over the bowed-headed cornfields.

So at last Leon broke away from mankind. No loyalties remained to chain him. Hunger was ever his constant companion, but the untouched earth was kinder to him than the villages. Quickly he learned that a rustle in the silence meant a lizard or a snake and his movements became as swift as theirs in his hunting of them. He found hunting by night more propitious than by day, with bats and beetles and, along the river banks, rats and voles.

Hunger made him agile and cunning. His skin was nothing more than a draping over his bones, but still he was strong. His eyes grew bright again and his coat improved. He swam in the rivers, he rolled on the dusty earth, he gambolled through the corn. His tawny hair thinned out and began to shine.

When he came to a village he would hang about for several days, scrounging what he could from the rubbish dumps, making off with a chicken when the occasion presented itself. His method of chicken-stealing was usually infallible. He would pick on a bunch that scrabbled about on the outskirts of the houses, and, much as if he were herding sheep, creep up cautiously, imperceptibly edging them farther away from home and into the corn. They would flutter and cackle a little, but so patient and slight were his movements that before they could become aware of his intentions he would be off at a lope with a madly squawking hen grabbed firmly within his jaws, and by the time some woman had come to rescue her flock Leon would be half a mile away and out of sight.

Still he would not stop. The blood trail could be followed and, for all that his head would begin to droop with the weight of the struggling, wing-flapping bird, Leon would hurry for another couple of miles before finally deciding that he could safely stop and devour his prize.

3

All through the spring and summer Leon lived in this manner. He did not live well but he lived happily, the bitter resentment blown from his heart by clean winds, lost on the plains where no man came to molest him. At times he was almost a puppy again, stalking his shadow, or pouncing on rustling plants as if they were a prey to be dispatched. At night the moon exaggerated his gauntness and lit up his way across the hills. During the day the hot sun lulled him to sleep.

Only hunger ever drove him back to the villages. There were days on the plains when he could find neither hares, nor voles, nor even lizards, and he would search farther and farther afield until in the distance he would spy the ochre walls and red roofs of a hamlet. For several days he would hang about it, scrounging what he could from the rubbish, stealing a hen.

These occasional excursions did nothing to recall him from the wild life he had chosen. In every place he was driven away. No one ever called him or showed the slightest friendly interest in him. He instinctively kept away from Hilario's village, although many were the times that it had been within easy reach. The knowledge that his beloved master was not there kept him at a distance.

One day he heard something that stirred an eager memory within him: the faint jangling of sheep bells. Ears pricked, tail held high, he loped in the direction of the sound and from a hill-top looked down upon a small flock grazing lazily across the previous year's corn stubble, nibbling at the weeds that had sprung up and at the grass that grew along the banks between the different terrains.

A whine of excitement welled in his throat as he watched the ewes. They were untended and each one was hobbled, fore and hind legs roped together. There was a village not far distant from whence they had come that morning. Leon flopped down on the ridge to watch them. He was tempted to go down among them, just to be close again to the creatures it was his instinct to herd, but he was afraid that someone would come and drive him away.

He stayed there for a long time, tongue lolling, ears pricked, until he saw a woman come from the village and drive them back towards it, with a stick to urge on the stragglers. When they had gone Leon felt restless and some of his pleasure in freedom faded. The sheep reminded him of Nicolás and his life as a shepherd's dog, and again he was lonely, longing for some man to want him.

Several times he came to watch the sheep and he thought the woman had never seen him. But one day he learned that he was mistaken when she came in the company of a lad, pointing to the hill-top where Leon crouched silently. The lad had an air rifle and he fired it at the dog. He missed, but Leon took fright and fled, the unexpectedness of the action bewildering him but reinforcing his status as an ownerless, unwanted dog. The people feared him and, although he could not understand the reason for their fear, it affected him and made the gulf between himself and them wider still.

By their constant spurning of him they made him a vagabond and an outcast. He was wild because they made him wild. He stole because they would not let him eat.

Winter came and to keep himself warm Leon needed more food. The blood ran thin and weakly through his body and he was no longer carefree. The winds were not playful now but scythes that cut in long vicious strokes across the plains. For the dog there was no shelter. The ground was frozen, the streams were iced over and icicles hung from the reeds. There was no food anywhere for Leon, not even in the villages to which he returned constantly in desperation.

The women in the hamlets thought he was a wolf and were afraid because their husbands were away in the war and they had only lads and old men to protect them. Rusted shot-guns were brought out and filled with whatever could be found that would serve to keep him at bay. And Leon went back to the plains with their snow-capped ridges still hungry and ever more desperate.

He remembered the hobbled sheep that he had watched before the woman brought the lad to shoot at him. He returned to the place from which he had often looked down upon them and found that they were still there, thin and bony-looking, for all the dirty bundles of wool that straggled across their backs. Several of them had lambs shivering at their heels, weak-looking creatures that seemed incapable of surviving the winds and storms that still awaited them.

The dog watched them, his eyes glittering. The bones of his haunches stuck out of the deep hollows of his flanks and so great was his hunger that it overrode all other instincts he had once possessed. Gone was his desire to protect, gone was his memory of the shepherd's trust. The smell of the ewes was the smell of meat and he crept snake-like towards them, not losing his patience for all his hunger, so that the sheep were hardly aware of him and not even frightened when they saw him.

He picked out a lamb as his easiest prey, unhobbled and able to run. He drove it before him, insinuating himself between the lamb and its mother in such a way that neither was aware of it until he was in complete control. The mother called to the lamb and tried to follow. Leon drove her back to the flock, gently but firmly, then returned to his hazing of her youngling, pushing it farther and farther away until he got it beyond the ridge and out of sight of the village.

Once he had killed his first lamb and had tasted more meat and blood in one ravenous meal than in all his five years, it was both tempting and easy to kill again and again.

13: Juanjo

Juan José had never seen so much space before. He had
walked more than a mile from the village and, although it
was still within his sight if he turned his head, it was far
enough away to be insignificant and he could pretend that
it did not exist. So much walking tired him and he stopped,
squatting down against a bank of earth which acted as a
windbreak. He blew on his hands to warm them. He
hunched his shoulders and then sat still, hugging his hands
and arms against his ribs, suddenly aware of the immensity of
emptiness before him.

Juanjo was a city boy. He had been born in Madrid and had
lived all his nine years there, hardly stirring from its over-
crowded centre and narrow streets. The vista from his fifth-
floor home had been of dusty red roofs or of other buildings

as tall as his own. He had only been in the country, staying in his grandmother's village, for two weeks and until now he had hated every moment of it.

When he had set out on this morning to walk so far it had been with the intention of running away, of finding his way to the railway station and hiding on a train that would return him to Madrid and his mother. But after a mile and a half, feeling stiff with cold and hungry, Juanjo had stopped.

He could see right to the horizon. The earth was almost completely flat, brown and black and grey-looking, and what had only been a geography lesson before became reality when he saw how disc-shaped it was in the distance. The earth really was round as his Jesuit masters had told him.

He stared at the austere countryside, his brown eyes large with surprise and thought. He grew warmer away from the wind's constant tugging and his face no longer felt as though it would crack at the slightest movement. Running away at the end of September was not a good idea! To walk as far as the horizon would take him days and days and perhaps he would reach it only to discover a further interminable stretch on the other side.

The hopelessness of it suddenly overcame him. Tears welled involuntarily. He rubbed them roughly away with his sleeve as soon as he felt them but they rose even faster. His lips trembled and his heart felt as though it would burst. He allowed the tears to slide down his cheeks and then he put his head in his hands and, because there was no one to hear him, permitted himself to cry.

He cried because his mother had left him, because his father was in prison – a thief, everyone in the village told him – and because his grandmother obviously hated him. He loved his mother but could not forgive her for having left him there. For two weeks his heart had been heavy with pain, culminating in his attempt to run away and return to her, and now that there was no one to jeer at him, to overhear him, the stemmed tears flowed; the quietly breaking heart was silent no more.

He cried until he had no more tears left to shed, until his eyes were dry and burning, his cheeks hot. And then he felt better. He was no longer angry with his mother and he could at least challenge the stories about his father with which his grandmother and his cousins had taunted him. How could he have ever believed them?

Juanjo sniffed hard and wiped his runny nose on his sleeve. He was even beginning to like the bleak aspect of the plains. There were no dark, crow-like eyes constantly watching him as in his grandmother's house; there were no shouts of other children, teasing him. There was only merciful silence, merciful solitude. He began to think about his father.

The last time Juanjo had seen him was on his sixth birthday. He had brought the boy a pet rabbit which Juanjo and his mother had eventually been forced to eat, and all that the boy recalled was how fine his father had been in his uniform and how proudly he had afterwards told his friends that his father was a major. It had been a short visit, more than three years ago, and since then so many things had happened and the world had been so upside down that, apart from his daydreams, a photograph, and the questions he put to his mother, Juanjo knew very little about his father.

But he was not a thief, for all that his grandmother insisted on calling Juanjo 'son of a thief' whenever she was angry with him, which was at least twenty times a day. She shouted it everywhere in the village until all the children took up the refrain, 'Where's that son of a thief from Madrid?' If he had decided to run away it was because he could no longer endure the chant, which followed him along every lane and wafted from yards and outhouses, often faithfully copying the intonation of his grandmother. Even his cousin Fernando, two years his senior, as brown and as solid as Juanjo was pallid and frail, and who had offered him a semblance of friendship, resorted to the intonation and often led it.

Fernando was strong, ignorant and friendly in a bullying sort of way. Secretly Juanjo was afraid of his friendship, which could change to emnity in a second and return again just as rapidly, and tried to avoid him. The only person to be kind to him was his grandfather.

A flicker of a smile passed across the boy's face as he thought of him. What fantastic tales he told! And how he liked to tease his wife. Juanjo wondered how he had the courage to outrage her as he did, laughing at her scoldings to annoy her more, and he felt a kinship with the stubble-cheeked old man who wore a grubby black beret on his head from morning till night, never removing it, not even when he occasionally washed his face. He probably slept in it, too.

The smile faded. Grandfather spent most of his time with his donkey and was rarely in the house. He spoke to the donkey as if it were a person. He had only just bought it and it was blind in one eye. He had bought it from a gipsy; according to his wife the same gipsy who sold him a lame donkey the year before. But Grandfather had only laughed and told her not to interfere in a man's business. Buying and selling donkeys had nothing to do with women.

'And that's why they always deceive you. You haven't bought a healthy donkey yet.'

Grandfather let Juanjo ride the donkey. He learned to sit on its haunches, well to the rear. At first he sat on its back, in the middle, and when the donkey began to trot Juanjo found himself jogged up to the withers, on to the neck and in the next second he was sitting in the dust, the donkey looking down at him and waggling its ears.

Juanjo was growing cold again. The wind had changed direction and was swirling round the ridge of earth, freezing his legs. He pulled up his socks and stood up, no longer feeling quite so miserable. He would go back to the village and see if he could find his grandfather in one of the fields. Perhaps he could have another ride on the donkey. He stared once again at the land, spread out in every direction, leading seemingly to the edge of the world, then turned and set off at a run towards the village.

His socks had slipped again and his legs were scratched by the old, dry corn that still stood, ungathered through lack of men to do the harvesting. He enjoyed running through it, feeling it crackle under his boots, and he swept down a slight hill with his arms outstretched, imagining he was an aeroplane. He zoomed and swirled in preparation for a bombing attack on his grandmother's house and, as he turned rapidly about, his eyes registered the head of a dog watching him from the top of the hill.

He stopped and glanced upwards but the dog had gone. Perhaps he had imagined the pricked ears, the pointed muzzle and the ragged, lion-like mane.

He was near the village now and he spied his grandfather at a distance, digging in one of his fields. A fire was blazing near by, beside which stood the chocolate-coloured donkey, nodding its head.

2

The farmer was digging up a few potatoes for their supper that night. He took a long time over the task, for, like his grandson, he was in no hurry to return to the village and his nagging wife.

'Where have you been?' he called to the boy as Juanjo came trotting up, red-faced and blowing hard. 'Your grandmother's very cross because you ran off so early. She wanted you to bring water and she had to go herself. You'll be in for a hiding when you get back.'

He said all this in a cheerful, philosophical tone, but, as the boy's face lost its animation, he winked and added, 'It's better that you stay with me for a while. There's no point in hurrying now. It's already too late.'

He drew Juanjo close to the fire, picked up a stick and poked at a few potatoes that were blackening in the ashes.

'Go and get a few more sticks,' said the man. 'Then these potatoes should be about ready.'

There was a stack of dead vines in the next field that his grandfather had been cutting. Juanjo brought back an armful and watched the man place them carefully in the flames which roared for an instant, devouring the dry fuel. Then they crouched down together and the farmer pulled two potatoes out of the ashes with the stick.

'Your grandmother's expecting us back for a meal,' he said, 'but I don't think we'll bother. She's in a bad mood. There's plenty of potatoes and here's a skinful of wine. That's enough for a bony thing like you and an old man like me.'

He winked again and Juanjo grinned. All his unhappiness was forgotten. He drew closer to the fire to warm himself and his grandfather said, 'Where have you been?'

'There's nowhere to go.'

There was a long silence while they waited for the potatoes to cool and the grandfather carefully pulled off the burnt skin.

'I saw a dog,' remembered Juanjo. 'At least, I think I did.'

'Did you now? That's interesting. What kind of dog?'

Juanjo shrugged. 'Just a dog. I only saw it's head. It looked like a lion almost. Perhaps it was.'

'Perhaps.' A glimmer came to Grandfather's eyes. 'Did I ever tell you about my adventure with a lion when I was in America? I was only a lad, sixteen or seventeen, and it so happened that . . .'

For the next hour or so the old man related his adventures to Juanjo. He went from one tale to the next and each was more incredible than its predecessor. The donkey drew nearer and hung its head over its master's shoulder. It nibbled at the charred potato jackets and seemed to listen to the tales as atten-

tively as did the boy. The sun slowly faded from the sky
and the horizon glowed redly, breaking up the clouds into
curved bays and islands. The earth reflected its brilliance and a
few puddles turned to silver in its rays.

Juanjo watched the sky and the earth. Madrid and his
mother seemed a long way away. Even the blows his grandmother was saving for him had lost their significance. His
grandfather had stopped speaking at last and the only sound
to break the still silence was a muted sheep bell and a few
faint bleats.

The donkey stirred and sighed.

'Yes. You're right,' Grandfather suddenly said to it. 'It's
time to go home. Come on, boy. We can't put it off any
longer.'

He swung Juanjo up on the donkey's back and walked
beside him. The sky grew darker as they jogged back to the
village and the houses became a part of the earth. There was
a glimmer among them here and there as women began to
light oil lamps and candles.

The boy's tranquillity suddenly deserted him. He grew
restless on the donkey's back and the man at his side said
gruffly, 'Don't worry. You'll get used to her, the same as I
did.'

As they reached the village they stopped to talk with a
group of men who were gathered in the plaza. Juanjo was
sleepy and hardly listened to them. He stayed on the donkey,
apart from the group, and thought about his grandmother.
Then his grandfather returned and he held squirming and
mewing in his rough hands a tiny ginger and white kitten.

'Take it,' he said, thrusting it at the boy. 'They were going
to throw it in the river. But don't let your grandmother see it.
Keep it in the barn with the donkey.'

Juanjo pushed the shivering kitten, skeleton thin, inside his
jacket. Apart from the rabbit his father had given him long
ago, he had never possessed an animal. Perhaps there would be

something to enjoy in this village after all, if only he could keep from annoying his grandmother and learn to ignore the taunts of the children. In his grandfather at least he had an ally.

He put his hand inside his jacket to feel the kitten, no longer struggling and crying, and a smile formed slowly on his lips.

14: The kitten

'It took you a long time to dig potatoes,' began the grandmother as they sat down at the table in the dimly lit kitchen.
Until then she had not spoken nor even given any sign of
awareness of their return to the house.

'The boy's been helping me and we decided to eat a few
potatoes while we were there. There was a good fire, wasn't
there, son?'

Juanjo nodded, hardly looking up from the plate of chickpeas that his grandmother had slammed down in front of him.
There was a chunk of pig fat in the middle of the plate and he
pretended that it was a fortress which the chickpea soldiers

had surrounded. The only good thing about being with his grandparents was that there was always plenty to eat. For three years he had been constantly hungry, subsisting on the lowliest of diets, and until now he had forgotten how delici-ous the stewed pig fat could be.

'Afterwards we stopped in the plaza,' went on Grand-father, hoping to console his wife a little.

'What were they saying?' snapped the woman. Even though she was curious, she was incapable of being pleasant.

'Nothing. They were talking about that dog again. You know, the one that's supposed to have killed so many chickens and even sheep. Clementino lost a sheep only a few weeks ago. It just disappeared, and he reckons it must have been the dog.'

'Even a dog can't just make a sheep disappear. There must have been traces.'

Grandfather shook his head. Juanjo looked up from his besieged fortress. He was remembering the dog he thought he had seen that morning.

'They're saying that it must be a dog trained in herding sheep and therefore he can march off a chicken or a lamb without any fuss. Then, when he's a good way off, he kills it.'

'No dog could be as clever as that on its own,' snorted the woman. 'More likely there's a master giving him orders, someone who keeps the chickens for himself.'

'Anyway, Clementino wants us to go out and look for it one of these days. He's got a shot-gun and the first dog he sees out in the fields he's going to kill.'

'What else were they saying?' asked the woman. She was tired of the dog. It was not an interesting subject. She and her husband had no sheep and their few hens were kept in the yard so they had nothing to worry about.

'Elsa del Pozo is going to be married in December.'

'What's the hurry? Her young man only came back from

the war a few months ago. And with all the harvests ruined they can't afford it.'

She grumbled on about people's extravagance for a long time while the other two at the table ate their meal in silence. Juanjo was hoping that he would be able to sneak away to the barn to see his kitten. When his grandmother was not looking he dropped a bit of fat and a few chickpeas into his concealed hand and hid the mess in his pocket. The kitten would be hungry.

'Did they say anything else?' she asked at last.

'Yes. But I can't remember what it was.'

Grandfather winked at Juanjo, but the boy's answering grin froze upon his lips as he saw the woman's sharp black eyes upon him.

'I haven't forgotten you, lazy good-for-nothing,' she cried at him. Her features twisted with rage and Juanjo was frightened. She looked just like a witch with the black mourning clothes that reached to her ankles, her pointed nose and her eyes of jet.

'Now I remember,' broke in her husband, drawing her from her target. 'They were saying that Espinoso's son is coming back.'

'That boy! You mean the one that went off to Madrid before the war to be a doctor? But they said he was dead a long time ago.'

'Well, they must have been mistaken. Espinoso's had a letter. He's coming back at the beginning of December. Espinoso himself was there. He had the letter in his hands. He was almost crying.'

The grandmother gave a scornful grunt. She had no time for sentiment. She had borne eleven children and at the earliest possible moment had sent them out into the world to look after themselves. Her youngest child had gone to Madrid at the age of twelve and she resented very much having to look after this grandson of hers now. And all because her eldest daughter had married a man who meddled in politics. She felt no compassion for the boy's loneliness. Selfish to an extreme, incapable of either giving or receiving affection, she looked upon him only as a nuisance to be endured with as little grace as possible.

When the meal was over Juanjo sneaked out of the kitchen to the barn. He had put the kitten in a straw-lined crate and it was still there, mewing at the sight of him, hissing as he put his hand in the box to pull it out. He drew back with a start, the kitten's venom frightening him, and while it watched him with flattened ears and bared teeth, crouched almost flat in the straw, Juanjo pulled out the chickpeas and the bit of fat and dropped them under the kitten's nose. The kitten pounced ravenously upon the dusty offering and in a second it was gone. Juanjo wished he had brought more, but there was nothing else and if he went back to the kitchen now his grandmother would see him.

He stayed talking to the kitten for a long time. There was an oil lamp in the stable which his grandfather had shown him how to light, and the gloomy shadows it flung on every side disturbed him. The rustle of the donkey's hooves in the straw, the scratching of a mouse, all played on his over-wrought nerves and at last he took the courage to defy the kitten's spitting fear and pulled it out of the box into his arms.

After a moment the kitten began to purr, pressing its paws into his chest, sucking at his jersey. With the small live thing crushed up against him, needing him, his imagination was soothed. He stroked his fingers gently over the tiny cat's back and head and began to talk to it softly.

2

Juanjo learned to keep out of his grandmother's way as much as possible. She did not send him to school and no one seemed to bother very much about him at all. He wandered about the village at will and spent as many hours as he could with his grandfather. The other children he hardly got to know as he was a shy boy and they looked upon him as something of a curiosity, a city boy whose ways were different to their own. He would share their games when his grandmother let him, but he was so uncommunicative that they soon tired of him and left him to his own devices. After a while they no longer remembered to tease him and his cousin Fernando even offered condolences when he knew that Juanjo had been punished by his grandmother.

The boy kept the kitten a secret from everybody. Only his grandfather knew of its existence and he brought it food whenever he remembered. Grandfather forgot that Juanjo was only nine years old and he related to him all the news and scandals of the village. Sometimes he took the boy to the tavern with him and bought him a glass of wine, and Juanjo would sit at the table and listen to the talk of the farmers, feeling one of them, secretly very contented.

The main item of conversation was the killer dog. Clementino, the shepherd, had lost two ewes in five weeks and he had a cousin in the next village who had also lost sheep in a similar fashion.

'And last year it was the same,' he said. 'I didn't lose any – it's the first time the dog's been in this district, I think – but my cousin had several lambs stolen and he also knows of other shepherds who tell him the same. And this apart from all the people who've lost chickens! I tell you, when I go out with the flock I carry my shot-gun with me.'

'That dog is too clever to be caught so easily,' said another. 'He's probably been at it for years and knows more about sheep than you do.'

'We should organize a proper hunt for him,' insisted Clementino, but the idea was received without enthusiasm. Most of the men had been away from the village for the length of the war – three years – and they were behind with all their tasks. Their fields had remained unploughed and untended for too long. There was no time for dallying.

'Put a price on his head,' suggested someone. 'Then you might get some results.'

Clementino pulled a face, but then he said slowly, 'With lambing time coming up within a couple of months it might not be a bad idea at that. I'll think about it.'

They discussed the dog, sometimes jokingly, sometimes seriously, nearly every evening. And when they were not talking about the dog they were mulling over the only other item of interest in the village, the return of Espinoso's son, Hilario, when everyone had believed him to be dead. Juanjo found this conversation less interesting than that of the dog. He knew nothing about Hilario and hardly listened to the voices about him, concentrating on his own thoughts instead.

He still had not surrendered the idea of running away from his grandmother and returning to Madrid. But he knew that it was no good walking as on the previous occasion. It was both too far and too cold. He needed money for the train fare; he needed someone who would take him as far as the nearest big town, which was Valladolid. Juanjo recalled the dog he had glimpsed but once. It had been a big dog and it had disappeared so rapidly that no doubt it was the one the shepherd sought.

If Clementino were to give a reward he, Juanjo, would find the dog, and he would ask the shepherd to take him to Valladolid and give him the money for his train ticket to Madrid. It was very simple, so very simple that Juanjo never doubted for an instant its possibility.

Then Grandfather was speaking at his side. The subject of the dog had come up again. Juanjo listened more closely for he had thought them still to be discussing Hilario. Grandfather said, 'Hilario had a dog, don't you remember? That big mongrel wolf dog that Don Agustín wanted. What became of that one, I wonder? It disappeared from the village at about the same time as Hilario.'

'He took it to my sister-in-law. She was married to a shepherd. That dog was a marvel with sheep.'

This was Hilario's second brother-in-law speaking. There was silence when he had finished. Everyone was considering his words carefully.

'Has he still got the dog?' asked Clementino at last.

The man shrugged negatively. 'I don't know. She lives a a long way away.' He named the village. 'We don't see much of her. But it would be against that dog's nature to harm a sheep.'

Clementino snorted. 'To a hungry dog a sheep is food. Don't try to tell me any different. Of course I'll offer a reward and if it turns out to be Espinoso's dog he can pay it.'

3

The very next morning, while his grandmother was down at the river with the washing, Juanjo took one of the blankets from his bed and slipped unobtrusively away from the village. He first of all collected the kitten from the barn and pushed it well down inside his jacket to keep it warm, and then set out to look for she fugitive dog, determined to seek for it every day until he found it. When he was well away from the village and there was no one to see him he stopped and put the blanket round his shoulders, as he had seen the shepherd do. It was heavy and clumsy, but it kept off the wind, and soon, with the kitten hot against his ribs, he began to feel comfortably warm.

He went from ridge to ridge, his eyes half shut as he strained them in an effort to see as far as the horizon, and the wind blew against him. There was not even the shadow of a dog, nor an imprint in the earth of its passing. He wondered if he had imagined the dog he had seen as he swept aeroplane fashion down the hillside, but no, it had been too vivid for that. He shook off his doubts, hugged the slipping blanket closer and wandered about for another hour, until hunger began to gnaw at him and he had to return home.

He left the kitten in the barn before going into the house. His grandmother was waiting for him at the door and his hope of returning the borrowed blanket without her knowledge was in vain. She grabbed him by the shoulders, screamed that he was a thief and a good-for-nothing just like his father, and gave him half a dozen blows about the ears. The good food, for which his mother had sent him to the village, almost choked him as he tried to swallow and it was salty with his tears. He refused to tell his grandmother why he had taken the blanket and was even more determined to run away from her as soon as possible. If only he could find the dog!

He looked for it every day. While the other children were in school, chanting sums and prayers, he would be far away on the plain, keeping himself warm with an old sack he had found in the barn, always with the softness of the kitten against his ribs. The kitten grew rapidly for all that it was half starved. It dug its claws gently into the boy, kneading and purring, sucking at his shirt as it had once sucked at its mother. Juanjo often put his hand inside his jacket to stroke the bony creature. It was the only thing he had to love now and he drew great contentment from its presence.

His only fear was that one day his grandmother would discover it in the barn. He always hid it in the box where first he had kept it, when he could not have it with him, but he knew that his grandmother hated dogs and cats and anything that had no specific use. It was probably why she hated him too. He was just a burden to her, as she had so often reminded him, eating, always eating, and his mother paying nothing for his keep.

October passed. The land looked more bare than ever but Juanjo was not afraid of its emptiness. The brown and ochre-yellow terrains were warm to him, accepting him. The only bleakness was when he had to return to the village, fearfully entering his grandmother's house. He had almost given up hope of ever finding the dog and was beginning to think that it must indeed have been a dream that he had ever seen it. Even the shepherd, Clementino, had stopped talking about it and seemed to have lost no more ewes. Often Juanjo forgot that he was supposed to be looking for it and he would find a sheltered spot where he could sit and draw out the kitten, letting it play with his fingers and throwing small stones for it to chase after.

But one morning when he stepped outside the door of his grandmother's house he noticed that the village was astir with news. From the patio he had a good view of the main square, and there were a number of people there gathered into a scattered group, all either talking or listening. In the centre was Clementino and he was shouting with excitement. Juanjo saw his grandfather among the crowd and he dashed down the muddy lane to join him.

'What's happening, Grandfather?' he cried, tugging at the man's rough hand.

'Hello! What are you doing here? I thought you were still in bed.'

'Well, I haven't had breakfast yet. What's happening?'

'Clementino almost lost another sheep.'

Juanjo's eyes opened wide. If the dog was not already caught now was his chance!

'Tell me!' he demanded, exasperated by the old man's slowness.

'Nothing to get excited about, young fellow,' the farmer laughed. 'And if your grandmother finds you down here at this time of the morning, and without your jacket, you'll be in trouble.'

Juanjo grimaced and begged his grandfather to get on with the story.

'All that happened was that the dog came right up to the

place where he corrals them for the night and was marauding about the walls. Clementino's dog started barking and he rushed out of the house with his shot-gun. He says he must have hit the dog, but as it was about two o'clock in the morning and very cold he decided against chasing after it.'

'He didn't kill it?'

'I don't think so. But he doesn't think it will come back any more.'

'Then he's not sending anyone to search for it? There won't be any reward?'

The grandfather understood at once the boy's tone and expression, so much longing and disappointment were expressed in both.

'Here comes Clementino. We'll ask him.'

Grandfather hailed the shepherd and put Juanjo's question to him. Clementino, draped in a thick grey blanket, for he was on his way to take out the sheep, looked down at the small boy who hoped to gain that very vague reward, and he thought to himself, 'Well, why not? If the boy can find the dog he'll be doing me a favour and I'll finish him off once and for all.' A few sweets or a couple of coins would be all that he was wanting.

He smiled and said, 'Of course. If you can find the dog and lead me to him you'll get the reward. I give you my word.'

Juanjo thanked him and promised fervently that he would do so, that very morning if he could. He rushed back to the house and it seemed a good sign that his grandmother had not noticed his absence. She put a large bowl of bread and milk before him and it steamed into his cold face as he ate, warming him. He gulped it down as quickly as he could, grabbed his jacket and rushed out of the house, not even caring that later he would be in trouble for not first gaining permission to go, and such was his hurry that he did not even think of taking the kitten with him.

He returned a couple of hours later, cold and discouraged.

As usual, he had seen no trace of the dog. Perhaps he had been looking in the wrong direction, but he could not understand how a wounded animal could disappear so completely and leave no trace. He had been so assured of success on setting out, so certain that it would not be necessary to endure more than a day or so more in his grandmother's house, that he could hardly find the courage to return.

He went to the barn first, suddenly remembering the kitten, and as he opened the door he knew that something had happened to it. With rising dread he rushed over to the box where it was kept, saw it upturned and empty, and almost stopped breathing as fear filled his heart. He looked cursorily about the barn, calling it but knowing full well that he would not find it there, and then he went to the kitchen and sat pale-faced at the table.

His meal was cold on the table, a cap of grease forming over it, and his grandparents had almost finished eating. They both stared at him, the man with compassion, the woman with harsh satisfaction.

'Where have you been?' she said. 'Rushing out of the house without a word. Is that a way to behave? And deceiving me, too, as usual. At least, I suppose that cat was yours? And what have you been feeding it on, I'd like to know? Do you think that in these times there's food to spare for a cat?'

Juanjo twisted the fork in his fingers. He could not speak.

'Anyway, it's dead now,' she added. 'I don't want cats breeding fleas in my barn.'

Juanjo stood up abruptly, hardly knowing what he was doing. He heard his grandfather say, 'You shouldn't have done that, woman. He hasn't a thing of his own,' and then he rushed out of the house, feeling that he would surely die too.

His sobs were loud and wild and a woman in the street tried to stop him as he dashed by her, struck by his distraught appearance. He averted her grasping hands and darted down an alley between the houses. He wanted only to get away, to be alone, never to have to come back. The village was behind him within a moment and when he realized that he was on the open plain he doubled his pace and flung himself headlong across the rough furrows, stumbling, tripping, not even noticing when he fell.

He ran until his lungs were tight with pain, until every breath he took cut through him like a saw. Then he tripped yet again and fell to his knees. He stopped there. He could run no more. He put his hands on the ground and leaned on them, his head bowed between his arms. The earth was cold and hard It was feelingless beneath him.

Juanjo stayed like that, panting, for quite some time. The perspiration was beginning to freeze on his head and inside his clothes and he began to shiver. He looked up and saw not far away, almost a part of the earth from which it had sprung, a tiny hut which he had never noticed before. He got up and forced his now unwilling body over the last long stretch that would take him to it. The wind shuddered through his shirt and his teeth began to chatter. By the time he had almost reached the hut he had to bow his head against it and struggle the last remaining yards.

The hut was made of stones and mud, and its roof was a tangle of dried grass, withered vines and straw, kept down with boulders. A shepherd had built it a long time ago and it was just what Juanjo needed now, dark and silent and far away from people. He crouched down to pass through the low, narrow doorway, and it was not until he was inside and sitting on the earthen floor that he realized that he was not alone. In another corner, staring fearfully at him, was the dog.

15: Hiding-place

The dog and the boy looked at each other for a long time. Leon was already accustomed to the darkness and could see quite well; Juanjo found himself with clearer vision in each passing moment. The boy's first reaction was fear. Within a fraction of a moment he remembered that this dog was a sheep-killer, hunted by men with guns; that he was probably dangerous, might even attack him. And in the next moment his fear changed to elation. He had found the dog! He would get the reward! He could escape at long last to Madrid! But still he made no movement for the fear returned almost immediately. If he moved, the dog might jump on him, and Juanjo hardly dared breathe.

Leon was as frightened as the boy. For so long had he been an outcast, and then a fugitive, that even this rather small human was enough to freeze him into fearful immobility. Where there were boys there were men. Perhaps within any moment a man would enter the hut also and he would be lost. He was intelligent enough to know that he was guilty of a serious crime that no man would forgive, not even his beloved Hilario who was almost nothing more than a vague remembrance in his subconscious, but in hunger and lust and the knowledge of his own strength and cunning he had been careless of this until now, when he was no longer strong and had forgotten to be cunning in his search for shelter.

His ears twitched back and forth as he watched the boy, listening for footsteps outside which would tell him of a man's approach, but there was no sound and some of his panic faded.

Juanjo watched the dog's ears and saw how they changed the expression on his face. When they were pricked he was quite a handsome dog and looked harmless enough. When they flattened, and the eyes stared balefully at him, he was reminded of a wolf, like the ones he had seen at the zoo.

Juanjo considered what he must do. He rejected the idea of trying to take the dog back to the village with him, certain that he would refuse to come and might attack him into the bargain. Therefore he must ensure that the dog did not escape from the hut. But how to keep him here when he had no string with which to tie him and nor was there a door that he could shut? He sighed. The problem was a difficult one. Then he wondered why the dog had not tried to run away. Perhaps it was not even the one he sought but some other from the village that had taken shelter here. No, it must be the right one. No village dog would come so far alone.

He automatically clicked his tongue and Leon suddenly pricked his ears. It was a questioning look and Juanjo forgot that the dog was supposed to be dangerous. He clicked again and snapped his fingers. The dog was alert and almost eager. He no longer looked so much like a wolf.

'Hello,' said Juanjo. 'What are you doing here?'

They were the first kindly words that anyone had directed at Leon in almost four years. They sounded strangely to him but they touched at something deep within him. A hidden memory? Or perhaps even a dormant hope? In his miserable state he needed someone to befriend him, he needed a human who cared, but experience had taught him to be wary of human treachery and he did no more than prick his ears and watch the boy's movements carefully.

Juanjo stretched out his hand. It did not quite reach the dog but he was afraid to go any nearer. Leon stared at the hand for several seconds and then stretched out his muzzle and sniffed at it carefully. It smelt as any boy's hand might smell and there was nothing to cause him to fear.

Juanjo continued to hold out his hand, forgetting that a few minutes earlier he had been afraid of the dog, and Leon nosed it carefully, desires, fears, instinct and knowledge, all fighting each other. He wanted the boy to be friendly, but no one had been kind to him since the shepherd had gone away. He wanted to surrender himself to this boy, but too many people had driven him away or tried to trap him for him to have any confidence in this latest one, small though he was.

He whimpered softly, wriggling slightly, afraid to surrender unwilling to deny. Eventually his need conquered and tentatively his damp tongue licked out over the boy's fingertips and his plumy tail moved slightly over the floor.

This was all Juanjo needed. Within an instant he was beside the dog, caution forgotten. He began to stroke the dog's head and spoke to him as he had spoken to the kitten. Leon cringed from his touch. The last person to come so close had been Rubio, whose hands had always hurt, but there was the memory of the shepherd's children and he could not defend himself against this boy.

He tried to shrink away and whined his distress, but Juanjo caressed him more, determined to show this fearful dog that he meant him no harm. Then Leon rolled on his back, surrendering himself in the only way he knew how, his dark eyes doleful as they gazed into the boy's face. Juanjo was delighted by the dog's move, for it was surely a sign that he wanted to play. He began to pat Leon's stomach and chest and, as no pain came with his touch, the dog began to grow in confidence also. He rolled upright again and allowed the boy to stroke and pat him as he wished, and now and again his tongue licked the boy's fingers and his tail wagged.

Juanjo remembered that the dog was supposed to be wounded but he could see no injury nor feel any dampness that might suggest blood. He began to doubt again that this was indeed the chicken killer. Then he stumbled over Leon's back legs and the dog let out a series of sharp yelps that frightened Juanjo.

'What's the matter? What have I done to you?' he cried, and the dog licked all over his hands and caused him great delight.

It was gloomy in the hut for Juanjo to be able to make out the dog's injury, but it convinced him once again that this was indeed the dog he sought. He must lose no time in racing back to the village and finding the shepherd. If he hurried he could bring Clementino here before the dog had a chance to escape or, even if it should run away, it would not be able to go far and it would not be difficult to find him again.

As he suddenly remembered his purpose, he drew sharply away from Leon. He could not be kind to him and then betray him. The dog felt Juanjo's withdrawal. He could not understand it but he knew enough of human beings after seven years to know that they could offer their hand one minute and their boot the next. He drew back to his corner and contemplated the boy with eyes that were no longer questioning nor eager. They expressed a wisdom that was beyond the boy's own.

Juanjo went to the door of the hut. The sky outside was grey-looking, suddenly overcast with heavy clouds. Even as he stared at it a big raindrop landed on his nose and startled him. Then a dozen splattered down in front of him, and within a moment the dozens had become hundreds, the hundreds thousands. They splashed on the dark, dry earth, making it darker still in rapidly growing patches.

Juanjo wore only a light jacket that was too small for him.

He knew he would be soaked before he reached the village, even though he ran all the way, but a sense of urgency overcame reasoning and, without even looking back at the dog, he set off at a swift pace across the open land, exhilarated by the unexpected rain.

Leon limped to the doorway of the hut and watched him go. The rain streamed down on the boulders that held its roof in place and drops began to seep through the thatch, falling with a pattern of thuds to the earthen floor. Leon pricked his ears, listening to the rain, watching the boy. And when Juanjo was a good distance away, almost lost in the greyness that was descending over the land, Leon also left the shepherd's hut. He limped laboriously in the opposite direction to the boy, not knowing what shelter he might find but afraid to linger in a place which could so easily entrap him.

2

Juanjo went directly to the shepherd's house. His clothes were stuck to him when he arrived there and Clementino's wife exclaimed in horror at the sight of him.

'What are you doing in such a state?' she cried. 'Haven't you a home to go to?'

She pulled him into the warm kitchen and stared at him. Juanjo ignored her incredulous gaze.

'Is the shepherd here, please?' he asked.

'What do you want him for? And surely it could wait. Surely it wasn't necessary to come out in this rain? You'll catch pneumonia.'

'It's important,' insisted Juanjo, wondering why all women bothered about such small details. Even his mother was guilty of this and she was the most perfect woman he knew.

'Well, he's not here. You'd better leave a message and I'll tell him when he comes in.'

'Where is he then?' cried Juanjo, hardly able to hide his impatience and beginning to shiver a little also.

'Out with the sheep. What is it you want?'

'Nothing.'

'Why don't you go home and change your clothes? By the time you've done that he might have come back. I don't suppose he'll stay out long if this rain keeps up.'

Juanjo nodded. It was easier to agree, although he thought of going to look for him in the fields. He was already so wet that a bit more would make no difference. He certainly could not return to his grandmother like this. She would not let him out again and would give him a hiding into the bargain.

The woman opened the door. 'Make sure you go straight home,' she warned him, and Juanjo thanked her politely and promised.

Instead he wandered round the alleys for a while, kicking at stones and jumping the rivulets that formed in the runnels down the centre of the rough streets. The rain was streaming finely now and he was very wet. He did not know where the shepherd might be and realized that there was no point in going to look for him. He would just hang about until he saw him come home. The alleys were deserted. Everyone was indoors except the children who were at school.

Juanjo found himself near the rubbish dump. He decided to look over it as there were interesting things to be found there sometimes, old bird cages or bottles and the sort of junk to arouse the curiosity of any boy. Everything was very wet, of course, and hardly worth picking up. He turned a few things over with the toe of his boot, his hands in his pockets, his arms hugging his ribs. And then he saw a bedraggled bit of ginger-and-white fur. His heart seemed to turn over and he thought he would be sick. He ran to pick up the kitten. It was stiff and cold and wet in his hands, looking and feeling nothing like the little creature that had nestled so often against his breast, purring and sucking at his clothes.

A feeling of hatred towards his grandmother was overwhelmed by one of helplessness. She refused to let him be fond of her; she scolded him when he went about with his grandfather; she tried to destroy his belief in his father and she wanted to keep him apart from the rest of the children in the village. Even this weak little kitten she would not let him have. He could not understand why and there was no way of trying to either soften her or battle against her. She would never let him have anything, whether it were a kitten or a dog or a bird in a cage.

The long streaks of rain on his face mingled with his tears. He held the kitten against him, trying to warm it, almost afraid of its stiffness. Perhaps it was not really dead. Perhaps he could still bring it back to life if he could keep it warm.

He took it to the barn, glad to find that the donkey was there alone. He filled the kitten's box with fresh, dry straw and laid it carefully down, smoothing its soaked body with his hands. As he did all this he suddenly thought of the dog. Soon it too would be dead. Clementino would take his shotgun and this time he would not miss. The dog would be dead and its body would be thrown somewhere to grow stiff and cold in the rain, just like his kitten.

He remembered the pink tongue licking warmly over his fingers.

Resolutely he pushed the thought away. Clementino would give him the reward. The reward would take him to Madrid. He would escape his grandmother and he would ask his mother to give him a kitten and to tell him the truth about his father.

His teeth were chattering but he hardly noticed. He thought the shepherd must have returned home by now and decided to call at the house again. He was about to leave the the barn when he stopped. He could not bear to leave the kitten alone there, so cold and wet. He found an old sack that smelled of potatoes and earth and carefully he laid the kitten on it and wrapped it up. There it would be warm.

He held the sack in his arms, covering it with his hands so that the rain would not reach the kitten, and as he made his way along the alley once more he saw the shepherd not far away, followed by a flock of hurrying, noisy sheep. They turned off into a stone-walled corral behind the shepherd's house and by the time Juanjo was at the door, Clementino had finished penning them and joined him there.

Clementino made Juanjo take off his clothes and sit close to the kitchen range with a thick blanket wrapped about him. He saw that the boy pulled the bundle of sacking close to the fire too, but said nothing. His wife heated up some soup left over from the midday meal and she gave a bowlful to the boy and another to her husband. When they had drunk it and sat silent for a while, watching the flames, Clementino said, 'Well, what do you want? Is it about the dog?'

Juanjo nodded.

'Go on then. Have you found it?'

'What reward are you offering?' returned Juanjo. He could not forget how the dog had licked his fingers and rolled on its back.

'What do you want?' Clementino was secretly amused by the boy's business-like manner and seriousness, but would not let it show.

For a moment Juanjo could not answer. He wanted it so much that he hardly dared speak. When at last he voiced his request the words came out in such a rush that the shepherd could hardly credit what he heard.

'Take you to Valladolid! Buy you a train ticket to Madrid! But do you realize what you're asking of me? I'll have the Civil Guard after me if I try to do a thing like that.'

'You won't do it, then?' said Juanjo, trying to control his despair. 'You won't even let me have the money?'

'First, I can't do it and, secondly, I haven't that much money to spare. Times are hard, boy. You must know that.'

Juanjo dropped his head. He did not want the shepherd to see his tears and was fighting to control them.

'What have you got in the sack?' said Clementino, but Juanjo could not answer.

The shepherd got up and unrolled the sack, finding the dead kitten in the centre.

'What did it die of?' he said.

Juanjo forced his voice to obey him. 'My grandmother killed it,' and then his sobs broke loose and he could no longer even try to disguise them.

Between sobs he blurted out all his misery to the silent and sympathetic shepherd and when he had finished crying the wife gave him another bowl of hot soup, although it meant that there would not be enough for themselves that evening. Clementino tried to console him and even assured him that his father was not in prison for being a thief.

'He's only in prison because he was on the losing side in the war,' he explained. 'Why, if I'd not been on the winning side perhaps I'd be in prison now instead of him!'

Both the shepherd and his wife cheered up Juanjo as much as they could while his clothes steamed themselves dry on the line over the fireplace. They made him share their evening meal and, while they were eating, the woman discreetly carried out the sack and its bundle to a place where the boy could not find it. She also ran to the grandmother's house and told her that the boy was with them.

It was late and still raining slightly when at last Juanjo was able to put on his clothes again, still slightly damp and warm from being ironed, and bid the shepherd and his wife good night.

At the door Clementino suddenly remembered the killer dog.

'Did you find him after all?' he said.

Juanjo hesitated for a second before answering.

'Not yet.'

16: Companions

It rained for two days almost unceasingly and the grey and
black clouds hardly moved in the heavy sky. Juanjo, kept
indoors and under his grandmother's eye the whole time,
could not disguise his restlessness. He thought constantly of
the dog, wounded, hungry and alone. He thought of the soft
tongue licking him gingerly and he wanted so much to be
with the dog that he would have risked his grandmother's ire
had he been able to escape her. Above all there was the fear,
the almost certain knowledge, that when he returned to the
hut the dog would not be there.

After two days a strong wind began to blow and the clouds
moved, breaking into islands between which gleamed the sun
in patches of blue. Juanjo was allowed to go outside and he
saw that mud was everywhere, thick, yielding, hidden in

places beneath long stretches of puddles. The sun glittered on the water, turning it to silver. In the distance it looked like snow.

Juanjo stood in the soggy strawed yard, contemplating the scenery. Then he saw the big earthenware basin in which his grandmother prepared the pig's food. There was a stodge of beans and lentils and potatoes. He saw a broken plate in the rubbish bucket beside the bowl and the two things together made him realize that the dog would be hungry.

The woman was upstairs making the beds and sweeping the rooms. Rapidly Juanjo took the plate, dug it into the pig's food and filled it as much as he could. Then he was out of the yard and in the alley behind the house so that he could not be seen, and soon he was hurrying across the soft fields, his boots plastered and his socks splattered, hoping – hoping so fervently – that Leon would be there, waiting for him.

The hut was dark and damp and empty. Juanjo put down the plate and walked about outside, scanning the fields and and horizon. He called, 'Chucho!' – the name given to all nameless dogs in Spain – and began to scale the slight slope behind the hut, searching hopelessly. Several times he called but there was no sign of the dog, or even a paw mark in the dark earth.

It was cold and the damp had seeped through his boots into his socks. He decided to return to the village and it was as though the distance had doubled itself on the return journey for the heaviness of his heart seemed to weigh down his feet.

The next day Juanjo returned to the hut and to his joy found the plate empty. Some animal had come to eat the food. It might have been the dog. He looked about with eagerness. Where could an animal as large as that dog hide? There was neither tree nor boulder and yet somewhere near he must be hidden, perhaps watching him even now.

The last thought encouraged Juanjo. He would bring more food. He would bring it every day until at last the dog trusted him and showed himself. And he wandered about for a long time calling, convinced that the dog was listening.

The days went by and Juanjo kept to his decision. There was not always food to bring and then Juanjo would scrounge about in the rubbish and, even if he found only an old bleached bone, he would take it just to show the dog that he cared and had not forgotten him.

It was on the fifth day that Leon suddenly appeared out of nowhere, standing with head erect, his thick tawny mane giving him a regal appearance, his ears pricked. The boy's heart seemed to jump within him and he could hardly breathe. He could not even call but stared unbelievingly as Leon came unhurriedly towards him on three legs, watching his face constantly with alert dark eyes. As the dog reached him, Juanjo held out his arms, his face shining with joy.

Leon bowed his head and pushed it against the boy's knees, the wagging tail denoting his silent pleasure. The boy began to pat him all over and Leon caught Juanjo's hand gently between his teeth, pulling it towards him. Juanjo knelt down to caress him more easily and Leon's long tongue slobbered over his face. He put his front paws on the boy's shoulders and Juanjo put his arms round the dog. Like this they stayed for several seconds, two outcasts discovering a need for each other. The dog looked at the boy, his eyes searching, intense, and then Juanjo put a hand on each side of Leon's head. Holding the dog thus, he said earnestly, 'Will you stay with me?'

Leon, in answer, licked the tip of his nose.

2

There began a wonderful time for Juanjo. While the fields were still ashy with frost in the middle morning, he would be running across them, leaving his prints in the silvery greyness, looking for the wolf dog who would be waiting for him, ears pricked, tail wagging, somewhere near the shepherd's hut.

Sometimes he brought the broken plate laden with food. Other times he came empty-handed, but the dog always greeted him with gladness, if not exuberance, and Juanjo forgot that he had wanted to run away from the village, so happy was he to be with the dog.

He also forgot that Leon was supposed to be a sheep and chicken killer, a thing he could not believe anyway for the dog was always so gentle with him, even when he took a hand in his mouth as he sometimes did.

The two companions would sit together near the hut. Sometimes Juanjo would speak and fondle Leon. Sometimes Leon would lick the boy's face and hands. But mostly they just stayed together, silent, close, contented, Juanjo with a hand resting on the dog's back. Juanjo would think about the dog, seeing how raggedly thin he was in spite of the bits and pieces he managed to bring him. The dog's hair was dry and dull and often his nose was parched and hot. For all that he knew nothing about animals, Juanjo could tell that Leon was sick and that the sickness must come from the injured paw which the dog would not let him touch.

It was not the shepherd's bullet which had harmed him, for that had gone over his head, but a sliver of broken glass which had embedded itself in his pad a fortnight before when he was scrounging about a rubbish heap in one of the villages. He had licked and gnawed at it endlessly but so fine was the crystal that no efforts of his could dislodge it. Little by little poison was setting in. The foot was hot and swollen and caused him to whine while sleeping.

Juanjo wished he could bring his grandfather to look at it, sure that the man who loved his donkey so much would know how to treat an injured paw, but he knew that the dog would not come to his grandfather and was also afraid that the man might give away his secret. He was talkative and would forget any promise to keep silent, and then Clementino would come with his gun. He could not bear that to happen and when he sometimes thought of it he would cling to the dog, pressing his face against him and thus dispel his dread.

Leon did not think or analyse as Juanjo did. He was happy to have the boy come to him, glad to have someone who cared, but he knew that he did not belong to the boy nor the boy to him. Their companionship was limited to the hour or so they spent together in the fields. It was all Leon wanted of the boy and all that he could give him. When Juanjo went away he was lonely, but he would not follow him.

3

Juanjo's freedom and happiness were not to last. His grandmother seemed to sense the pleasure he found in spending all his hours alone on the barren plain and, without wondering the reason for it, disapproved and decided finally to send him to school. At any other time the boy would have rejoiced at the idea for, until he had the dog for company, he was often lonely and felt an outcast. But now he could not concentrate on any lessons, already behind those of his age group, nor even join his companions' games with much gusto, thinking of the dog, wondering how it would be faring without him.

It was dark by four in the afternoon and school was not over until five. On Saturday afternoons his grandmother kept him busy about the house and on Sundays they went to church and ate the midday meal so late that again it was dark before he could escape. The days dragged by, each one anxiously awaited and unhappily lost, and he thought of the dog growing hungry again and desperate. The teacher scolded him for his absentmindedness and the boys lost interest in him for the same reason.

Only his grandfather seemed to sense that something was worrying him and one Sunday afternoon, when they were gathering dead vines for fuel and loading them on the donkey's back, he saw how Juanjo constantly watched the horizon and said, 'What are you looking for? What do you expect to see?'

'Nothing,' replied the boy.

He dared trust his grandfather even, knowing that no one in the village would be sentimental about a sick and hungry dog, especially if it were reputed to kill chickens and lambs. Grandfather loved his donkey because it was his. He cared nothing about his neighbours' animals.

The farmer did not believe him but was not anxious to pry. Perhaps he already guessed the boy's secret but preferred not to know for fear of becoming involved. He seemed to forget the boy's preoccupation for he suddenly said in the cheerful tone he always assumed when repeating village gossip, 'They say that Espinoso's son will be back some time next week. That'll be something to look forward to, especially as no one knows whether to greet him as a hero or suspect him as an enemy.'

'Why?' asked Juanjo.

He was growing more interested in this mysterious personage, so much talked about these days in the village, for he had learned that Hilario had owned a dog and that Clementino at least believed it to be the same one that he sought to kill, the one he himself had grown to love.

Grandfather chuckled. 'Because no one knows whose side he was on in the war. He's behaved very mysteriously has that one, and everybody thinking him dead a long time since.'

'Does it matter? About whose side he was on, I mean? After all, the war's finished now.'

'Perhaps it doesn't, but there's plenty of people who still think it does.'

Juanjo secretly hoped that the mysterious Hilario had been on the losing side, as had his father. He felt an outcast among the people here who, for reasons he could not understand, weighted his shoulders with his father's transgressions.

He finished laying out the dead vines in a neat bundle, his head suddenly racing with ideas, his heart filled with hope.

His cheeks felt hot and he hid his face from his companion, afraid that his secret would show, but the farmer was also bending over the vines, chuckling softly to himself although Juanjo did not know why.

Hilario returned to the village the following Thursday. School had just finished for the morning, so that Juanjo was among the crowd that gathered avidly about his house and along the alley leading up to it. He came in a most unexpected fashion, in Don Agustín's motor-car which made only rare trips to the village these days through lack of petrol. Don Agustín sat beside him in the back seat, pretending to be unaware of the unashamedly curious faces, and the chauffeur forced the unwilling car through the ruts and mud with an expression of disdain on his coarse features.

Juanjo was disappointed in what he saw when the two men got down from the car. There were perhaps five seconds during which Hilario acknowledged the villagers' presence with an embarrassed smile and a few nods of his head, and Juanjo saw only a pale-faced young man in a shabby suit that did not fit him properly before he disappeared into the house and the arms of all his relations. Any hopes that he had entertained of being able to rush up to him, tell him about the sick dog and encourage him to save its life, dwindled painfully. And perhaps it was not his dog, after all.

He slipped away from the alley, kicking listlessly at a stone, apathetically bereft of inspiration. He did not know quite how he had expected Hilario to be, but his imagination had dwelt vaguely on a bright-eyed, eager young man, capable of taking charge and solving problems. This one looked weak and exhausted and was no doubt completely disinterested in animals of any kind. He was no robust villager able to wrestle with a stubborn mule or dirty his hands pulling a stone out of an ox's hoof. A stray dog would make him think of fleas and rabies and he would no doubt encourage Clementino to be rid of it.

Juanjo, disillusioned, took an almost savage pleasure in tearing his hopes to pieces. By the time he had circled all about the village, kicking the same stone before him, he could see the dog, skeletal and ravening, dragged before the unforgiving shepherd for execution. He could see it in every detail, imagining himself present, and he saw the dog turn its mournful, hopeless eyes upon him, begging for a salvation that he could not give it. The eyes were large and dark and desperate, not in a wild way but only through fear, and Juanjo, seeing them, cried out, sharing the dog's agony. 'No! . . .'

The agony was his own, not the dog's, and now Juanjo was running across the unploughed furrows, almost sobbing for the dog of his imagination. He grew hot with fear and exertion, arriving stumbling and painfully breathless at the shepherd's hut. He almost fell through the low doorway and for seconds was completely blind in its darkness. He crouched panting, looking from side to side, and gradually the corners came vaguely into being, with a scattering of soft feathers in one of them.

Juanjo took some of them into his hand. They were downy and stuck to him. The bigger ones were bedraggled and chewn. He took them outside and saw in the daylight that they were not very old. They were still quite pretty, brown and speckled. He sighed. He hardly expected to find the dog still waiting for him. Almost two weeks had gone by since last he had come here, but he would have rather not found this proof of the dog's culpability. He could excuse it, knowing how hungry Leon must be, but no one in the village would forgive. And where was he now? Hunting again? Another chicken or a sickly sheep?

He looked about, seeing nothing against the dark soil, and he called hopelessly, hardly expecting the dog to be near nor even to come if he were. While he waited, he pulled up a few sods of cold earth, carried them into the hut and crumpled them over the feathers, hiding them as well as he could. The place smelled of chicken and the air was sour. Juanjo no longer wanted to stay there and he went outside again, not knowing what to do.

The dog was there, waiting for him as though nothing had changed! In a way nothing had, for all that they had not seen each other in a fortnight. The only change was in the dog's appearance, for Leon was almost defeated now, his body scorched by the fever of poison which would have its way for all he fought it. He showed no pleasure at the sight of the boy but Juanjo knew that the dog was glad to see him. He knew it by the way the dog had responded to his call.

Leon limped past Juanjo into the hut. When Juanjo entered the dog had already curled himself up in a corner, his head stretched out on his front paws. He no longer even tried to clean the injured paw, for it was too painful to touch and immeasurably swollen.

Juanjo sat down beside the dog and gently passed his fingers over Leon's head and muzzle. The dog's ears moved slightly and he sighed deeply. He let the boy fondle him without further sign and Juanjo stayed there until his stomach reminded him of the lateness of the hour. He was quite happy now, squatting down beside the dog, and would not have left him had it been possible to stay.

At last he rose, gave the dog a last pat, wished him good-bye and promised to return as soon as he could. Leon's ears twitched at his words and the eyes watched him as he crawled out of the hut.

When he was alone again, he fell asleep. He slept throughout the rest of the daylight hours and the hut quickly grew dark, long before the sky was completely overcast. He began to dream and whimpered often, and late at night he woke for a while, feeling as lonely as he had once felt as a tiny puppy crying for Hilario in the darkened kitchen of the house. He felt afraid, without knowing why, and he wished that the small boy who had befriended him had not gone away.

17: Memories

Don Agustín's obvious approbation of Hilario's actions, whatever they had been, was enough to encourage the villagers to look upon him as one of them and not one of the fallen enemy. Bit by bit rumours spread around as to his activities during the three years in which he had been lost even to his own family, and Juanjo heard them through his grandfather and exchanged stories with the boys at school. For at least a week no one talked of anything but Hilario, the women at the stream, their hands red and swollen with the coldness of the water, the men at the tavern, the children as they played.

Of Hilario himself little was seen. He was shy of appearing in public and made only one token appearance with his father at the tavern the night following his return.

Rumours had it that he had learned all the doctoring he knew in the crudest ways, tying up shattered limbs, bandaging blinded eyes, probing for shell splinters, in the trenches surrounding Madrid. And if this meant that he had been with the enemy, it was hastily overlooked and excused by saying that, after all, he had not exactly been a fighting man and took no active part in any battles. Certain it was that in his three years away he had studied little theoretical medicine and as yet needed much more grounding in subjects such as chemistry. He had indeed been wounded, not at the beginning of the war, as his parents had mistakenly been informed, but almost at the very end when a hand grenade that killed the patient he was attending, so shattered his senses that for six months afterwards he lay in a stupor, knowing neither who or where he was, nor even that the war had ended.

When eventually he recovered and, after convalescence, was well enough to return home, he was sent back to the village in style, and Don Agustín had received a lengthy telegram from his nephew at the hospital encouraging him to treat Hilario with respect.

And so the pallid, anxious boy, who had gone away from home for the first time almost four years earlier, returned a man in experience if not in years, and Juanjo, hearing the story bit by bit, began to review his former hastily drawn conclusions and wonder if this weedy-looking fellow could indeed be stronger than the element-hardened villagers who had known no suffering but their own.

Perhaps he could not handle a mule or an ox, but surely he would understand and sympathize with the sufferings of a dog? But then he wondered if, having witnessed so much human suffering, he would have grown callous to the feelings of mere animals. And Juanjo struggled with his doubts, wishing to find an opportunity to talk to Hilario, but almost afraid to look for it.

He might never have found the courage to speak to him

had he not gone to visit Leon once more. He played truant from school in order to do so, haunted by his last sight of the dog, gaunt and listless and obviously ill. He also remembered the chicken feathers and wondered unwillingly if Leon would have killed yet again. How could there be hope for him if he had?

It was a sunny day when Juanjo set out for the shepherd's hut instead of the classroom. Some of the boys saw him and shouted to him, but he ignored them and went on, hurrying to keep himself warm, for it was a cold brightness in the sky. The frost was like ash over the land and there was snow on the ridges. He was happy, thinking of being so soon with the dog, and when he was out of sight of the village he let himself go, first a galloping horse, snorting and bucking, then a glider floating in the wind currents like the big crows that shadowed the sky that morning. He had only just noticed them.

He remembered what his grandfather had told him about the crows, vicious scavengers who cleaned the plains of dead or sickly animals and were not averse to attacking lambing ewes or the newborn lambs themselves. He watched them with almost hypnotic aversion, soaring with grace in the blue-white sky, dipping, swirling, ominously black. He realized suddenly that they were more or less within the vicinity of the shepherd's hut and this caused anxiety to surge within him. Had the dog killed a sheep this time and was it this that drew them? He began to run, all pretences forgotten.

It was not a sheep that Juanjo found stretched out beside the shepherd's hut. It was Leon and it was hard to tell from a distance whether the dog were alive or dead. The boy flung himself over the last short lap and within seconds was kneeling down beside the fallen animal, disbelief keeping fear and grief still at bay. What had happened to him these last seven days? Oh, why had he not come before?

The dog was not dead. Indeed, his eyes opened instantly as he felt the boy's nearness and heard his voice. They stared

up at Juanjo as if in gladness to see him there but the tongue
was too dry to lick a greeting and the whole of the exhausted
body burned.

There was only one thing to do, fetch Hilario, and the boy
stood up decisively, all doubts and hesitation forgotten. But
first he must get the dog to the safety of the hut. He could not
leave him to the crows and could not imagine how Leon
had come to desert in the first place what was obviously his
den.

As well as he could, and not without difficulty for the dog
was heavy in spite of its gauntness, he gathered Leon into his
arms and stumbled with him to the hut, half dragging, half
carrying him. He pulled him inside, smoothed his hands over
him and uttered a few soft words. Then he was off with all the
speed he could muster. With the black shadow of the crows
behind him, never had the village seemed so far away.

2

Hilario was a person for whom Juanjo felt an instant admiration. All doubts concerning him immediately fell away as he
told his story in a confused avalanche of words, for Hilario
was not a person to ask time-delaying questions. He listened
almost in silence, only nodding his head occasionally, and his
mother's disapproving exclamations were as if non-existent
as he asked Juanjo to lead him to where the dog lay hidden.
He followed the boy with rapid strides, his face expressionless,
and Juanjo's only way of knowing whether he cared about
the dog or not was by the fact that Hilario came.

Across the ice-hard fields they went and Juanjo's heart
surged with excited gladness. He had forgotten for the
moment the urgency of the occasion, convinced of Hilario's
ability to save Leon, convinced too that the dog was his. And
when they reached the hut and Hilario had pulled the dog out
in the daylight again, there was no doubting it. The until now
impassive young man cried out with all his heart, 'Leon!' and

the dog, rousing himself from a semi-conscious state at the cry, thrust himself upon Hilario and would have gone wild with joy had he possessed the strength to do so. He contented himself with broken whines, welling up from an overfull heart; and pawed weakly at the man's legs, his eyes staring intently into those of his master.

For a moment Juanjo felt bitter and sad. The dog had forgotten his existence and no longer needed him. He would have turned away and gone back to the village, but suddenly Hilario called to him and said, 'We shall have to get him back to my house. It looks as though I shall have to cut open almost half the leg to get the poison out.'

'Will he get better?' asked Juanjo, screwing up his face at the horrible vision these words presented.

'I don't know. It should have been seen to much sooner and he's very weak.'

For a moment more Hilario fondled the dog and held it close to him and then he stood up and was business-like again, all emotion vanished. He pulled Leon into his arms and Juanjo was surprised at his strength, for Hilario was as thin as a corn-stalk.

Later, back in the farmer's kitchen, he was even more impressed by Hilario's ability as he watched, wide-eyed and curious, the swiftly made preparations; hot water, cotton wool, some rags torn into bandages, a razor sterilized in alcohol. Even Hilario's mother was interested and proffered assistance. Even the farmer himself, grumbling anew about the dog, was keen to see his son's performance and proud of his unfussy competence.

The farmer was drawn to act as assistant, clamping one strong hand over the dog's muzzle and weighting down its shoulders with the other. Hilario's mother promised to keep Leon's hindquarters still. Juanjo, almost forgotten, watched in silence. At one time he thought the dog was dead, so still did it lie on the kitchen table in spite of the razor and Hilario's probing of the putrid paw. But he did not often look at the dog, his attention mostly drawn to Hilario's face, impassive, cold. Had he not heard that heart-felt cry on the plain he would have thought that Hilario cared nothing for Leon.

At last Hilario was satisfied. He dressed the leg with care, gave the word for Leon to be released, and carried the almost immobile dog to a place close to the fire, placing him on a blanket and covering him with another.

Leon was cadaverous, his head off the blanket and stretched on the warm stones of the hearth. Never had he looked so weak and skeletal and everyone stared at him for several minutes, thinking that at any moment he must die. Hilario left them to watch while he busied himself burning soiled swabs and disinfecting the razor, and only when everything was clean and as before did he come back to Leon and kneel beside him.

Juanjo still watched, wishing he could be there in his place, but, as he watched the man's lips move in almost silent words and saw the dog's ears twitch feebly in response, he knew that no one could replace Hilario. If Leon lived it would be because Hilario was beside him to pull him through, and not because Juanjo loved him and cared.

Hilario's mother broke the silence.

'Do you remember,' she said unexpectedly, 'when you first brought him here? He was dying then and you put him out on a blanket in the sun.'

Hilario said nothing, but he remembered. In those minutes, while he watched over the dog, willing it to live as he had willed many a dying man in the past few years, he was recalling memories of those days with his dog, carefree days which had belonged to another world. He had thought that there was no connection between the boy of that time and the young man that he was now. His imagination, overwrought with nightmares of unforgettable visions, suddenly grasped out to that far-distant time, that other life, when his only worries had been his studies and a dog had filled his days with pleasure.

While he absently stroked his hand over Leon's semi-conscious body he remembered sunny days when they had stopped somewhere beside a field of swaying corn, crushing the poppies and cornflowers that grew riotously over every green bank, he to peruse his books or the infinite arc of sky and earth, the dog to watch his face. And the nights of fishing by the light of the moon, and the sharply cold winters helping Nicolás with the sheep.

Memories tumbled over each other; of rescuing a bleeding, blind scrap from the clutch of a crow; of his bare feet hot under the weight of the faithful puppy while he sat at a table in the priest's house studying; of chasing hares; even of his fear of Don Agustín and the cold tramp home without his constant shadow behind him.

All these things filled him with a joy that he had forgotten. They were as real as his nightmares, but suddenly stronger. The dog lying in exhausted sickness at his feet was again the key to all that he had found beautiful in life, reminding him of a time before hideous things existed, of a time of love and innocence.

Hilario suddenly caught sight of Juanjo and the expression on the boy's face, one of wistfulness and pain almost, filled him with concern. He himself felt so glad, so new again, that he could not bear another's suffering now.

'How old are you?' he asked.

'Nearly ten.'

'And are you happy?'

Juanjo could not answer. It was a question no one had ever asked him. He dropped his eyes and twisted a leg, looking awkward and shy. Then, after a long silence while everyone stared at him, he said almost indistinguishably, 'Not very.'

'Then you must come here often,' said Hilario. 'The dog will make us both happy.'

18: A master to respect

It was not easy for Hilario to keep Leon. The shepherd Clementino was irate at the news that the killer dog's life had not only been saved but determinedly clung to. He had every reason for demanding the dog's death, and Hilario's father, irritated the past few months by the jibes that had fallen on his head – remembering still Clementino's threat in the tavern that he, Espinoso, could pay the reward for the dog's capture – was as much in favour of Leon's execution as any that demanded it.

He remonstrated angrily with his son, for once loquacious after a harsh scene with Clementino at the tavern, a scene witnessed by all and everyone hostile. In the tavern he defended his son's right to do as he wished with the dog but at home he denounced Hilario's determination as sentimental pig-headedness.

Hilario was stubbornly silent under his father's ranting. He could never explain to the unimaginative farmer his reason for clinging to Leon whether he had been condemned as a killer or not. And when Clementino called at the house one evening, together with several neighbours whose chickens had been mysteriously disappearing for some time, all demanding that Leon be handed over to them, he faced them calmly, the dog at his side.

'There's no proof of his guilt,' he insisted. 'You, Don Clementino, only saw a dog in the darkness. On a moonless night you couldn't recognize him among the half dozen other mongrel wolf dogs that roam about here. As for the rest, none of you have actually seen my dog go off with a chicken.'

'There's no proof that it wasn't him either,' retorted the shepherd. 'The fact is that he's the only dog in these parts that lives like a vagabond, out on the plain. Why should he hide like that if he has nothing to fear?'

'Because people have made him fear, people have driven him away and ill-treated him.' He almost added, 'People like you.'

Hilario had discovered the broken rib, healed now in its fashion, but proof enough of someone's ill-treatment of Leon. He would never know what kind of life his dog had had since last he had seen him but he knew that the dog was not a killer by nature. Only circumstances could have driven him to such extremes and he would not allow his dog to be condemned by circumstances.

'There'll be no more lost sheep or chickens, I promise you. Give him a chance.'

'Why should we?' answered a villager gruffly.

'Because . . .' Hilario's grey eyes were eloquent in their pleading. 'Because I need him.'

The words were quiet, intense. No man there, for all his ignorance, could disbelieve them. They stared at the thin-

faced man, with the still skeletal dog at his side, and then one
by one they found excuses for going home, muttering, 'We'll
see,' or, 'We'll think about it,' and similar phrases.

Only Clementino remained, stubborn, unyielding.

'That dog killed my sheep,' he said.

'I haven't the money to pay for your lost sheep,' answered
Hilario, 'or I'd gladly do so. Please, Don Clementino, be
patient. I'll show you one of these days what a good dog he is.
In fact, if you'll have him, when I return to the hospital I'll
leave him with you. He'll help you with the very sheep he's
supposed to have threatened.'

'Supposed! You admit yourself that he's guilty. And if you
give the dog to me I shall only kill him.'

'No,' disagreed Hilario. 'Not when you've seen how
clever he is. Feed him at least once a day and treat him as a dog
should be treated and he'll give you good service.'

The shepherd went away, unmollified, but puzzled enough
to let the matter rest for a while. He watched Hilario and the
dog together and saw how both improved in each other's
company, the former losing his pallid, morbid aspect little by
little, the latter growing strong and sleek and proud-looking
once again. And he continued to say nothing, waiting for
Hilario to fulfil his promise.

2

The rest of that winter passed rapidly, the dog and his master
recuperating together and Juanjo rediscovering happiness in
their company. When the boy was not at school, and the
weather permitted, all three went for long walks. Juanjo
talked. He talked as he had not talked for a long time, pouring
out all his unhappiness and fear to his companion who listened
attentively, said little, but consoled him just by caring. And
sometimes Hilario talked, telling the boy of his own childhood
in the village, reminding himself at the same time and finding
healing in the memories.

Leon walked between the two of them, handsome again now that he was cared for, the ruff of tawny hair thick over his shoulders and lion-like. He listened to the voices of both with a deep, calm pleasure that had begun to fill him as soon as he had been able to lift his sick head from the blanket and realize that once again he was in the house of the only human he could ever love. The time of fear, of desperation, of savage hunger was past, and he clung to Hilario, his eyes watching and anticipating his every movement.

When the fields were thick with snow and harsh winds drove along the alleys, Hilario and the dog stayed at home, warm in the lamplit kitchen. Hilario would muse through his books, a hand straying to the dog's head occasionally, finding comfort in his presence, and sometimes Juanjo would be there too, watching the dog or the flames in the hearth, not needing to speak.

The snow had gone and the fields were soft and brown and waiting for spring when Hilario eventually approached the shepherd. Clementino's flock had almost tripled with the new season's lambs, and it was not easy for him to keep them together for they could sense the spring as much as the birds and the soil and frisked all over the place like mad things, heeding neither dams nor shepherd in their delight.

Clementino knew nothing of Hilario's fear when he brought the dog to the shepherd. Juanjo had come too and was both sad and wondering. Leon saw the sheep scattered over the grassy ridges and his whole body tensed with anticipation. He looked up at Hilario, whining softly, and even his master could not know precisely what the dog's feelings were. What were sheep to him now? Woolly-brained beasts for his personal depletion, or in need of his protection?

The shepherd, the young man and the boy stood together on the plain and watched almost breathlessly as Leon, after one glance at Hilario, set off towards the sheep, ears pricked, head high, tail waving. They saw him approach in a wide circle, drop down suddenly and almost disappear, his colouring blending well with the earth.

Clementino drew in his breath sharply for the object of the dog's attention was a month-old lamb, lost-looking and bewildered, and unaware of Leon creeping insidiously up behind him.

The lamb bleated, its tail wagging. It suddenly saw the dog, but Leon's movements were too smooth to frighten it unduly. Leon crept another pace forward; the lamb backed two paces, watching the dog, almost hypnotized.

'Call him off,' cried Clementino, but Hilario held the shepherd back as he was about to run to the lamb's rescue.

'Watch!' he almost hissed. 'Just watch.'

Now the lamb was worried. It looked about for the flock, bleating again, and set off at a trot, watching the dog out of the corner of an eye. Leon, still half crouched, followed, gently driving so that the lamb could not be more than slightly afraid.

Its mother suddenly detached itself from a bunch of grazing ewes and came trotting to look for her youngling. When the two met, Leon dropped away and left them, looking about until he found three ewes that were grazing on a bank alone. These he also hazed back to their companions and, within half an hour, he had the whole flock compact and tranquil but respectfully aware of his presence.

The shepherd was perspiring, for all that it was cold and he had stood unmoving for so long.

'It's unbelievable,' he said. And then, 'But how can I trust him?'

'Just by putting your faith in him. He's an intelligent dog, Don Clementino, and he needs work. I must go back to the hospital and I can't take him with me. He needs a master he can respect and one who will appreciate him.'

The shepherd was silent, and Juanjo looked at both men. They had forgotten him. He might have known that his happiness could not last.

But then Hilario said, 'One favour I must ask of you if you decide to accept the dog. You must let this boy come and see him sometimes. If it hadn't been for him, Leon wouldn't even be alive.'

Juanjo grinned admiringly up at Hilario, his heart suddenly very full. Clementino looked at the boy.

'You deceived me,' he said admonishingly. 'You told me you hadn't found the dog.'

'Only because I loved him and didn't want you to kill him.'

Juanjo looked worried, his joy suddenly fading again, but then the shepherd laughed and ruffled his head.

'All right, I forgive you. You can come with me and the dog whenever that grandmother of yours will let you.'

Simultaneously, all three looked for the dog again. He was not far distant from them, having taken up a watchful position on a small hill from which he could overlook the movements of the whole flock. For the time being he had forgotten the existence of the men. The smell of the sheep was strong in his nostrils and it filled him with contentment. Gone was his lust to kill. Within him swelled only a desire to protect. It was in his blood, this instinct, and would be there till he died.

Hilario called him. 'Leon!'

Leon pricked his ears and turned his head in his master's direction. But he did not come running as Hilario expected. He stayed with the sheep. They needed him more than did his master.

The Brumby

Mary Elwyn Patchett

The Brumby of this story was a wild Australian stallion, born near the home of a lonely boy, and capturing his imagination with such intensity that he could think and dream of nothing but one day building up a herd of sturdy silver brumbies.

But to the Australian stockmen among whom he lived all brumbies were wild, vicious, untameable animals fit only to be hunted, and young Joey had to endure seeing his beloved foal grow up into a savage outlaw and finally a killer. Nevertheless his dream comes true in the end, although not quite as he'd imagined it.

Break for Freedom

Ewan Clarkson

Syla was a mink, and so dark brown she looked almost black. The cage where she lived was identical with all the others, except for one thing—there was a loose staple in the floor of her sleeping box. And that was how Syla escaped from the fur farm to find a new life, free in a remote valley on the edge of Dartmoor, free to hunt and fish and play, and also to face the dangers of traps or fierce animals, or the perils of the wild life which has no mercy on weakness or carelessness.

The author makes a fascinating story of Syla's year on the moor, and at the same time he tells us about all the other inhabitants of Dartmoor, the birds and insects, snakes and rodents, till the moor seems as busy and complicated as the greatest human city.

Ginger Pye

Eleanor Estes

Ginger Pye belonged to Rachel and Jerry Pye and he
grew to be quite a famous dog in Cranbury, because
of the clever way he tracked Jerry to school.

Then one day when dinner was over and Jerry had
gone out to play with his dog, Ginger had gone.
Of course everyone searched for him but no-one
had seen him, which was odd, since Ginger was so
well known. And who had let him out? There were
no holes in the fence, so he couldn't have got out by
himself. Jerry was determined to search for months
and months if need be, though all he had to go on was
a yellow-mustard coloured hat.

A Newbery Medal Winner.

The Custer Wolf

Roger Caras

One April five wolf cubs were born in a cave under a
tree stump. One was white, and men would come to
call him by a name that would live in history, for
this was the beginning of the legend of the Custer Wolf.

This wolf inexplicably grew up different from any
other. He was a beautiful but solitary animal and as he
grew it became clear that he killed for the love of
killing and terrorised a huge area round the town
of Custer for six whole years.

Sometimes he killed thirty cattle in a week, more than
he could possibly eat, and he took incredible
chances, yet he escaped every trap that was set and
every gun that was fired. Small wonder that the men
believed the white wolf was charmed.

If you have enjoyed this book and would like to know about others which we publish, why not join the Puffin Club? You will be sent the Club magazine *Puffin Post* four times a year and a smart badge and membership book. You will also be able to enter all the competitions. Write for details to:

The Puffin Club Secretary
Penguin Books
Bath Road
Harmondsworth
Middlesex